I0527360

Hiram Knight

Biography of Deacon James Allen

Hiram Knight

Biography of Deacon James Allen

ISBN/EAN: 9783337388997

Printed in Europe, USA, Canada, Australia, Japan

Cover: Foto ©Andreas Hilbeck / pixelio.de

More available books at **www.hansebooks.com**

James Allen

BIOGRAPHY

OF

DEACON JAMES ALLEN,

BY

HIRAM KNIGHT,

WITH

GENEALOGICAL REGISTER

AND

TESTIMONIALS.

Worcester. Mass.
PRINTED BY CHARLES HAMILTON
No. 311 MAIN STREET.
1889.

CONTENTS.

PREFACE.

It is highly proper, as well as natural, that a special veneration for the place of our nativity should be cherished. The scenes of our childhood; the kindly faces and cheerful words of those elderly people who greeted us when we were among the little school-children; the very land itself, its roads and by-paths, its woods and fields, its rocks and rills, and the greens upon which we gambolled may well be among our choice memories.

There, too, in some one or more of its sacred enclosures we visit and revisit in memory at least, the graves of parents, brothers, sisters, and perhaps of husband, wife or child, and looking around on either hand we read the names of associates and friends of our youth or riper years, making these places seem to us even as hallowed ground. We also feel and gratefully acknowledge a personal indebtedness to the place of our birth and childhood.

It is good for us to remember the virtues of parents and grandparents, and to realize the moulding influence which not only they, but other good men and women exerted upon us, directing us into paths of virtue and giving to us impulses towards right doing and noble endeavor.

The fact that Oakham was the place of birth and boyhood of the writer, coupled with his personal obligations to Deacon Allen, creates a desire to aid the recollections of the

2

sons and daughters of this goodly old town, who like himself were brought up under the influence of such men, and a desire (if possible) to secure the attention of the younger natives of the town, or their descendants, who, if at all, only remember the subject of this narrative as an old man who had passed his active life before they knew him, and who may therefore be inclined to feel that he was very little if anything to them because he was *old* when they were *young*, so that they have not been aware of much, if any, direct influence from him upon their own lives. But if they reflect upon the acknowledged indebtedness of their *parents*, whose lives were touched by his moulding hand, they may be able to see that through *them* even their *own* lives have been affected by *him* for good.

In the hope that the story of his life and labors, so far as they are set forth in the following pages, may not only remind the older people how much they were indebted to him and his co-laborers, but also serve as an incentive to nobler effort and greater fidelity on the part of the young, this little volume is respectfully dedicated to the Town of Oakham, and to her children at home and abroad by the author,

HIRAM KNIGHT.

NORTH BROOKFIELD, 1889.

TOPOGRAPHY.

THE town of Oakham, in the westerly part of the County of Worcester. Mass., is situated about sixteen miles west of the county seat (Worcester), and like the towns by which it is surrounded,—Barre, Rutland, Paxton, Spencer, North Brookfield and New Braintree,—its central portion is considerably elevated. Its surface is somewhat diversified and uneven, abounding in wooded hills and generally fertile hillsides and valleys, through which run numerous streams of limpid waters, so that its farms are well watered, and upon several of its larger brooks small mills were erected in the early days of its English history, and some of these streams still furnish water power for its home industries. Much of its soil is naturally productive, though by no means free from surface stones and rocks.

It was taken from the more ancient town of Rutland, and incorporated as "District of Oakham," June 17, 1762, deriving its corporate name, probably, from the kind of tree which predominated in its forests when its occupancy passed from the red to the white man, or, possibly, as some have believed, from a town of the same name in England. It seems to have been laid out into farms of the then prevailing size (averaging about one hundred acres) by its earlier white occupants, and these farm lines have remained as nearly unchanged as such divisions of the land have in the surrounding territory.

Many of its early white settlers came from the older and more easterly towns in the State, some, perhaps, from neighboring States and some from Scotland through the North of Ireland. Of the latter were the Crawfords and Bothwells, of which names the earlier and some of the later ancestors of the present generation lie buried in the old church-yard, very near where the meeting-house formerly stood, or upon their own farms in the easterly part of the township.

As in other towns in the vicinity the church with its "Godly Ministry" and the school-house received early attention. Its first church "was imbodied in presbiterian form Aug. 28, 1767, and Rev. John Strickland was ordained their pastor Apr. 1, 1768. He was dismissed by the presbytery and a vote of the town June 2, 1773. After Mr. Strickland's removal, the presbyterian church was dissolved, and a church on the congregational plan was imbodied June 23, 1773, and the Rev. Daniel Tomlinson was separated to the work of the gospel ministry among them, June 22, 1786."

Most of the early settlers were poor or of moderate financial means, and so much the more dependent upon their ability to labor as well as to endure hardships and privations.

Seventy-five years ago, notwithstanding the natural asperity of the soil, the town contained an average number at least of well fenced and well cultivated farms, many of which have continued in the hands of the same family names; some have passed to newer residents, some are in better condition than they formerely were, while in a few cases the once well appointed, well wooded and well tilled farms have fallen a prey to the avarice of sons or of strangers, have been divested of their wood and timber, the buildings gone to decay, very little now remaining to prove the industry, frugality and thrift of former owners. Like as in other farming towns the old has given place to the new, and though the inhabitants who have recently passed away and the few men and women now living in advanced age may have sorrowed as they witnessed these changes, and thought of former magnificence, they might, if permitted to look upon the present state of things, be forced to admit that upon the whole the new is as good and in some respects even better than the old. By the action of time and the laws of progress, old farm buildings, once the homes of contentment and comfort, around which have clustered so many sacred associations, are broken down or removed or forgotten; the perhaps sterile acres upon which very much labor had been expended because of their adjacency to the *home*, have been abandoned to pasturage or to a later growth of small wood; and also newer and better homes now stand where in former days comparative unthrift had been the rule.

NUMBER OF INHABITANTS.

According to the Colonial Census in 1765 (three years after its incorporation) the number of inhabitants of this town was only 270

In 1776,			598
In 1790, according to U. S. Census,			772
In 1800,	"	" "	801
In 1810,	"	" "	848
In 1820,	"	" "	946
In 1830,	"	" "	1,010
In 1840,	"	" "	1,038
In 1850,	"	" "	1,137
In 1855, according to State Census,			1,062
In 1860,	"	U. S. "	959
In 1865,	"	State "	925
In 1870,	"	U. S. "	860
In 1875,	"	State "	873
In 1880,	"	U. S. "	869
In 1885,	"	State "	749

Like other hill towns situated away from great thorough-fares where few special manufacturing industries have been permanently established, Oakham has had not only its gradual and earlier *increase* but its later gradual *decline* in the number of its inhabitants. Not by famine nor by pestilence nor by lack of general healthfulness has its population been diminished, but by a continuous exodus of its young men and young women who have been attracted to larger towns, to cities and to distant States and countries. About the time when the rearing of young men and young women destined to go from their native soil was fairly begun, the subject of this historical narrative came upon the stage of action. As a town builder, a teacher and a character builder he had few equals and fewer superiors.

James Allen, the only son of his parents, was born in Oakham, July 2, 1792, upon the farm now owned and occupied by Mr. Lewis N. Haskell, a little more than a mile south-west of the centre of the town. Of his parents comparatively little in detail can now be said, as there is probably scarcely an individual now living who was personally acquainted with his father, nor, perhaps, even with his mother, who survived her husband. The records show that his father was a deacon of the Congregational Church in Oakham from the time of its organization in 1773 till his death, a period of forty-three years. And the records at the State House show that he was a member of the House in the Legislature of 1805, and that he was a Justice of the Peace from 1802 till his decease.

It is no doubt truthfully recorded of him that he was ever active in promoting the interests of the town and the church. During the prevalence of the *spotted fever* in 1810 he gave his entire time to the care of the *sick*, committing matters at home and the care of the family to his eighteen years old son. And this he did upon the consideration that he was getting to be an old man (then sixty-six years of age), and if either might chance to become a victim to the terrible disease, it were better that *he* should take the *risk* and that the life of the son should be spared that he might care for the family.

There can be no doubt that James was religiously trained and instructed by his parents. His early opportunities for a school education were such as the common schools of his day afforded, and two years at the Leicester Academy, supplemented by his own earnest and persistent endeavors to gain knowledge by personal effort and study. In this he was aided by General Crawford.

After he was twelve years old his father gave him his choice between a college education and the ownership of the farm. He chose the former and in due time entered Leicester Academy to fit for college. At two different times his health failed him and he was compelled to abandon his choice. In his second year at Leicester he was a part of the time in the family of Mrs. Washburn, whose son Emory (afterwards governor of Massachusetts) was then seven years old. An older brother went with James to call upon some young ladies. He thus introduced him, "This is James Allen from *Oakham*." It was a cruel joke, for Oakham was not usually spoken of with much respect. "Out of the world into Oakham" had become a proverb. If in later years the town is spoken of with honor to itself, the change is in large measure due to the life and labors of this then tall and comely youth James Allen. He learned civil engineering or land surveying, which became one of his prominent occupations in after life.

From fifty to one hundred years ago were the times of *large* families of children, and as the farms and lands became nearly all occupied, and as water-power or other facilities favorable to its becoming a manufacturing town did not exist, whereby employment might have been furnished for its sons and daughters as they grew to man's estate, there was a constantly accumulating surplus population to be scattered abroad into other and growing communities within the State, or to make new homes for themselves and their children in other States or countries. The time was when by far the most important export of this goodly old town was young men and young women, and the same to a more limited extent is true even now.

And it is not aside from the purpose of this sketch to emphasize the *importance* which attaches itself to the home education and training of those outgoing as well as the remaining children of the town. There is a fitness of things, and there are laws of adaptation of means to ends and of ends to means which have their origin outside of or beyond the wisdom of man. If the towering cedar is needed for the building of the temple it is found upon Lebanon's mountain, where there is ample soil among the rocks to contain its roots and to nourish the tree, whose fibre is intensified and rendered more firm by its exposure to the mighty winds. If the sturdy oak is needed wherewith to lay the keel or to build the hull of the massive ship of commerce, it is neither found nor looked for in lowland thicket, but upon sparsely wooded hills where it has withstood the blasts of many winters and the trying winds of spring and autumn, causing it to root itself deep and wide and securing to itself integrity of fibre, that it may be the better fitted for the purpose it is destined to serve. So in the history of the human family, lofty intellects and sterling characters are needed. The exigencies of a State or nation may call for able and sterling men who are by the very necessity of the case to be found somewhere among the masses of the people, and not infrequently in the sparsely settled towns where they might have remained in comparative obscurity had not some exigency called them forth. Among the masses and even in small and obscure communities are often found military organizers and leaders, statesmen, teachers of the various institutions of learning and religion, philosophers, philanthropists, reformers. Nor do these do their work single handed or alone. What would be a general without an army drawn from among the masses; a statesman without appreciative constituents; a teacher without pupils; a preacher without attentive hearers; a philosopher, philanthropist or reformer without a sensitive and intelligent public mind to which they may appeal, or how can a man be distinguished as a town builder, and educator or character builder if he find no plastic material to work upon? The workman and his material must always coexist. The power to create from nothing resides only in the Divine Creator. Great men and good men made their appearance in this world before the fulness of time for the coming of the God-man; each from Noah down to the great but humble Nazarine, doing his appropriate work and leaving the world the better for his life. The like has been true since the Christian era, and doubtless will be true to the end of time.

When in due course of events our own nation sprung into life, its Washington and his faithful copatriots came forth from among the people. Later, the presidency had its Adams, its Jefferson, its Madison, its Monroe, its second Adams, and still later, its Lincoln, its Grant, its Garfield, and others of honorable mention. In the Civil War of 1861-65 the nation had its Grant, its Sherman, its Meade, its Sheridan, and other efficient military leaders too numerous to be mentioned. Thus has it ever been in the domain of religion, of learning, of science and art. Each honored name in his own time and work seems to have fitted into the divine plan of conducting the world's affairs, and in His own time and way of elevating the human race from a gulf of ignorance and sin to a mountain of knowledge and holiness.

Evil men have also arisen in all the ages whose energies and influence have been exerted for the destruction of that which good men have builded; and it is beyond human knowledge or wisdom to decide that their lives and labors have not also been comprehended in the divine plan. We may not be able so plainly to see the need of evil doers, but may safely conclude that to defeat or even to hinder the Great Ruler of the universe is utterly beyond their power.

Such reflections may lead us to infer that everything happens in its proper time and that each person lives at the proper time, every one in his *own* day and generation. From considerations similar in kind with the foregoing may we not safely conclude that the humble, but no less honorable and useful, subject of this sketch lived and labored *when* and *where* and *how* he could do the greatest amount of good?

To give an accurate list of the names of the heads of the growing families at any given date during the active life of Deacon Allen, in the education of whose children he acted a very important part, may now be impossible, but the insertion of the names to be found upon a tax list of 1827 may call to mind the property-holders and active citizens of *that* day, most of whom would be included as heads of families were such a list to be attempted.

TAXABLE PERSONS IN OAKHAM IN 1827.

Dr. Charles Adams.
Palmer Adams.
Cheney R. Adams.
Washington Allen.
Lysander Allen.
Nehemiah Allen.
James Allen.
{ James Allen for
{ estate of Isaac Stone, Jr.
Perley Ayres.
John Ayres.

Jonas Bellows.
Horace Bellows.
Anna Bell.
Nancy Berry.
Bethiah Black.
Lemuel Blake.
Reuben Bothwell.
Cheney Bothwell.
Rebeckah Bothwell.
John Boyd, 2d.
John Briant.
{ John Briant for
{ Daniel Boyden heirs.
James G. Briant.
Amos Bridges.
Jonas Brimhall.
John Broad.

Joel Bullard.
Adin Bullard (heirs of).
Moses Bullard.
William Bullard.
Josiah Burbank.
Patty Burbank.
John Burt.
Eli Burt.

Jonas Clapp.
Joseph Clapp.
Silas Clapp.
Edward Clark.
Lot Conant.
James Conant, Jr.
Charles Conant.
Harvey Conant.
John Conant.
Nancy Conant.
Isaac P. Conant.
Alexander Crawford.
Alexander Crawford, 2d.
Samuel Crawford.
Samuel Crawford, Jr.
William Crawford.
William Crawford, Jr.
Rufus Crawford.
Lauriston F. Crawford.
John Crawford.

Galen A. Crawford.

Galen Damon.
Adin Davis.
Polly Davis.
Zebulon Dean.
Elijah Dean.
Elijah Dean, Jr.
Blake Dean.
James Dean.
John Dean.
Josiah R. Dean.
Samuel Denny.
Cyrus Dunbar.
Joseph Dwelley.

Elmer Earle.

Ephraim Fairbank.
James C. Fairbank.
Ephraim W. Fairbank.
John B. Fairbank.
Harvey Fales.
George Fay.
{ George Fay for
{ Richard K. Shattuck.
Rice Fay.
Skelton Felton.
Peter Fitts.
Jesse Fitts.
Elisha Fitts.
Daniel Flint.
Perez Fobes.
Abigail Fobes.
Martin Forbes.
Benjamin Forbes.
Spencer Foster.
James R. Foster.
Susannah Freeman.
John French.
Bathsheba French.
Catherine French.
Asa French, Jr.
Freeman French.
Leonard Fuller.

William Gault.
David Goodale.

Eunice Goodale.
Samuel A. Goodale.
Rufus Gould.
Elijah Green.
Charles B. Green.

David Hager.
Isaac Hager.
Percival Hall.
Percival Hall, Jr.
John Hale.
Zenas H. P. Hale.
John Hammond.
Levi Harrington.
Levi Harrington, Jr.
Austin Harrington.
Warren Harrington.
Simeon Haskell.
Loring Haskell.
Thomas Haskell.
Nelson Haskell.
Daniel Haskell.
Joseph Hastings.
Sanford Hatch.
Samuel Henry.
Martin Howard.
Nathan Horr.

Joel Jones.
Isaac H. Jones.

Richard Kelly (heirs of).
Charles Keith.
William E. Keep.
Silas Knight, Jr.

Ezra Leonard.
Josiah L. Leonard.
Stephen Lincoln.
Stephen Lincoln, Jr.
Abner Lincoln.
Lucius A. Loring.

John Macomber.
Elias Marsh.
Elias Marsh, Jr.
Richard K. Marsh.
Amasa Maynard.

Samuel Maynard.
Ezra Maynard.
Francis Maynard.
John McCollough.
Stephen Moon.
William Moon.
Eliakim Morse.
Abraham Mullet.
Solomon Munroe.

Luther Noyes.
Luther Noyes, Jr.
Denny S. Noyes.
Timothy Nye.
Crocker Nye.
Salmon S. Nye.

Nehemiah Packard.
Perley Packard.
Jonathan Packard.
Solomon Parmenter.
Elias Partridge.
William Partridge.
Edward Partridge.
Thaddeus Partridge.
Daniel G. Piper.
Elihu Pond.
Frederick A. Presho.
William Presho.

Daniel Rawson.
Benjamin Reed.
Silas Reed.
Silas Reed, Jr.
Lewis H. Reed.
Joseph Rider.
Jepthath Ripley.
Zenas Ripley.
Russell Ripley.

Samuel Rockwood.
William Robinson.
Peter Robinson.
{ Peter Robinson for
{ Isaac Stone heirs.
John Robinson, 2d.
Abraham Robinson.

Lemuel Saunders.
Luther Spear.
Andrew Spooner.
Eleazer Spooner.
Caleb Spooner.
Calvin Stevens.
Otis Stone.
Charles Stone.
Justus Stone.
Betsey Stone.
Daniel Swan.

David T. Tenny.
Nathan Thayer.
William Thompson.
Fabien Tomlinson.
Samuel Tucker.
Luke Tower.

William Ware.
James B. Ware.
Ira Warren.
Lewis Wetherby.
Martin Weeks.
J. Chandler Weeks.
Hasky Wight.
Dorothy Woodis.
Polly Woodis.
Nathan Woodis.
Mariot Woodis.
Oliver Woodis.

NOTE.—Thomas Wetherell, who lived between Martin Weeks and Zenas Ripley, removed to Ware in 1827, just before this assessment list was made.

JAMES ALLEN'S MILITARY RECORD.

He belonged to Captain (afterwards General) William Crawford's *Grenadiers*. Appointed Sergeant, April 25, 1811 ; Ensign,

May 11, 1814; Lieutenant, January 27, 1815; commissioned Captain by Governor Caleb Strong May 17, 1817. This company was ordered to assemble at Knight Whitmore's Tavern in Oakham on Sunday, September 11, 1814, at 5 o'clock A. M., to march at once to Boston to repel the attack of the British, then threatened. In compliance with the order they then and there assembled, and after prayer (very long and solemn) by Rev. Daniel Tomlinson, and affectionate and tearful good-byes from loving parents and near friends, they took up their line of march; accomplishing the same in two days, arriving at Boston lame and stiff from their long and tedious marching, but soon thereafter through the thorough training of Captain Crawford they attracted the special attention of great numbers because of their proficiency in marching, their military bearing and training. They were known as the "*Tall Company*," also as the "*Country Haw Bucks.*" After about two months spent in and near Boston they returned home, having *seen* the enemy who did not dare to attack a city so well prepared to receive them. In the latter part of his life he received for this service two bounty land warrants, and after his death his widow received a pension.

Although he greatly enjoyed military life and service, yet for many reasons he thought best to resign his commission as Captain, which he did March 16, 1820. He was strongly urged to continue his military career, being assured of further promotion, but he did not think best to do so.

The older inhabitants will remember the Oakham and New Braintree Grenadiers. They were generally six-footers, and added to their very uniform height was the tall and imposing regulation cap or head-gear, heavily trimmed from behind and over the top with bear skin with its lustrous and flowing hair, also the tall, pointed and highly ornamented tin frontal, back of which was inserted a tall, black, red-tipped plume.

AS A FARMER.

In his youth he did not leave the old homestead, but came into its ownership either before or soon after the death of his father in 1816, when he assumed the care of his mother, who survived her husband about thirteen years. This was one of the well walled and well tilled farms and was kept in good condition so long as he continued its occupancy. He was a good farmer and a diligent worker upon the land, and became deeply interested and efficient (especially in his later life) in the cultivation of fruit-trees and the smaller fruits. As his public duties called him away more and more as the years went by he employed more farm laborers, who boarded in his family. No doubt the pressure of other business was one of the reasons which induced him to give up the farm in 1835.

AS A SCHOOL TEACHER.

This work he began when he was eighteen years old. His *first* school was upon the "East Hill" in 1810, and his *last* school was in the same place in 1852. His labors in this line for forty-two years were confined to his own town, extending to all parts of the town, as it is probable that he may have taught in each school district at some time in his life, or at any rate that many of the scholars living in the out districts attended his select schools in the centre. He early became a *model* teacher, and fortunate was the school which secured his services, and happy were its pupils, who as a rule cheerfully co-operated with him as their teacher. As compensation he received about the same amount that was usually paid in the respective schools; the minimum wages being about one dollar per day in the out-lying districts. Wherever there was a vacancy he was ready to fill it, even if it involved a foot journey of two miles each day and the consciousness when he reached his home at night that he had earned but a single dollar. In the central or larger schools in which he was usually employed he no doubt received more adequate compensation, but his work was as thoroughly and conscientiously done in the one case as in the other.

Though on the most intimate and familiar terms with all his pupils he always maintained *strict discipline* and secured good order and perfect obedience, not by resorting to corporal punishment for misdemeanors, which especially in the later years of his teaching he seldom found occasion to do, but by the *force of his own character*. He was often heard to say that no person was properly qualified to govern a school until he had learned to *control himself*. Being naturally quick-tempered and sensitive as to the dignity of his position as a teacher, his *own experiences* as well as observation may have confirmed him in such a conclusion.

He could usually keep his scholars from mischief or play by securing their interest in their proper work in which he was ever ready to assist and encourage them. Thoroughness in the studies, decorum in behavior, good order in school and consequent happiness were the *maxims* of his school-room. He opened and closed the school with brief religious exercises.

As the time arrived when Oakham, as well as its neighbors, felt the need of something more than the ordinary terms of district schools (which want gave rise to the establishment of high schools) Deacon Allen frequently taught fall terms of select or tuition schools in the centre of the town.

In the autumn of 1834 (the only time when he was under his instruction) the writer attended one of these schools in which there were about thirty of the more advanced scholars of the town, no less than five or six of whom went out from thence to become teachers themselves. Among this number was Levi Adams, who spent most of his time thereafter in teaching, until his early death in 1860, at the age of forty-three years.

AN INCIDENT.

About the year 1840, in the north-west district, an eccentric elderly man chanced to be appointed Prudential Committee (one of whose duties was the hiring of teachers). This man very seldom if ever attended church, or manifested any reverence for religion or much respect for religious people. Previously to and about this time opposition to religious teaching or prayer in school had found some sympathizers in this district, and, so far as is remembered, it is believed that the last teacher before this date whose custom had been to open and close with prayer was Colonel John Robinson, who taught school there several years before. This new committee man, regarding his own appointment somewhat in the light of a joke and thinking, no doubt, that he must do something odd in order to pay off his neighbors, hastened at once to Deacon Allen and hired him to teach the next winter term of school. As he met the boys he told them what he had done and warned them against throwing paper balls and doing certain other things in prayer time to annoy the teacher. The boys regarding his caution rather as a *suggestion* as to what *might* be done, prepared themselves for the occasion.

The day and hour of the opening came, and after a brief and pleasant introduction the teacher announced that the school would be opened with prayer, and to their great surprise these boys found that he could pray without *closing* his eyes or *fixing* them upon any particular object in the room. Being discomfited in their plans they thought best gracefully to submit to the *inevitable*, and in view of the pleasant and judicious manner in which the religious exercises were conducted, they soon began to realize their propriety, and with the other scholars they came to approve and to enjoy them.

AS ONE OF THE SCHOOL COMMITTEE.

In the early days of the writer as a pupil in the north-west district the School Committee consisted of Rev. Daniel Tomlinson, General William Crawford and Deacon James Allen. At the close of each term all three came together. Single visits were made at other times but oftener by Deacon Allen than by the others. On *examination* days the first two took the chairs assigned to them and remained in a dignified position while the school exercises were gone through with, but the Deacon moved noiselessly about all over the room, stopping to speak quietly with the scholars in their seats, commending them for good behavior and good work done, putting his hands upon the heads of the little ones and giving them pleasant words of approbation and encouragement. When it came to the speech-making Fr. Tomlinson opened very much in the solemn style of his pulpit ministrations, addressing the school no doubt in words of wisdom, but he made use of language which only a few of the scholars could understand. After him the majestic and commanding figure of General Crawford, incased in a blue coat with its bright yellow buttons, arose from his seat and poured forth a stream of eloquence which astonished his youthful hearers, but most of his classical language was beyond their comprehension, and if it did not minister to their present edification and enlightenment it caused the question to arise in many minds, Shall we ever know as much as General Crawford does? Then came Deacon Allen's turn to speak. He began down among the little ones and found much to commend in their behavior and recitations. Nothing which was commendable or praiseworthy escaped his notice, and if anything had appeared which called for criticism or rebuke he did not indulge in scolding to teacher or scholars, but in his inimitable way showed where and how improvement could be made. It is unnecessary to say that *his* was the speech of the occasion every time.

HOW HE CAME TO BE A MERCHANT.

In order to set forth all the accompanying circumstances and conditions bearing upon this subject some digressions seem to be necessary. Prior to 1834 Oakham had had its country store in the centre for an unknown number of years. As far back as the writer can remember it was kept by George Fay, subsequently by different parties, prominent among whom were E. W. and S. H. Skerry, and at this date it was kept by Potter and Rice, Mr. Potter being the manager. Previously to his day efforts had been made to establish certain kinds of manufactures. Mr. Ephraim Fairbank was the village blacksmith and reared a family of sons and daughters. Some of his sons first began the manufacture of window springs in the old shop on the corner south-west of the meeting-house. The work was done by hand processes aided by dies into which the steel for each separate spring was hammered. The push or thumb-piece brought into use in raising or lowering the window sash to the desired notch was made from sheet copper plated on one side with silver, out of which convex circles were punched, equivalent in size and shape to the largest round head upon the brass nail used in upholstery, and these caps were soldered to the protruding spindle of the spring. Agents were sent into various parts of the country to sell and set these then only known window springs. One among these agents was the late Perley Ayres, who operated in the middle and western parts of the State of New York. This manufacture for several years was understood as yielding a good return to the proprietors.

A little later on, some of these Fairbank brothers established what was then considered as quite a respectable straw bonnet factory, located upon or near the site of the dwelling-house of Deacon James Packard. In this factory several men and a much larger number of young ladies found employment for some time. The wagon and carriage business was also carried on to a considerable extent by Hervey and Humphrey, and by E. D. and E. Cheney. These efforts to establish manufactures upon the Oakham hill were contemporaneous with the establishment or early enlargement of the boot and shoe business in the Brookfields and other towns in the vicinity. But they did not long continue. These window-springs were superseded and the straw business was carried elsewhere, and the operatives who learned the latter in Oakham were drawn to other places for work ; and thus, instead of keeping the young people at home as it did for a time, and as no doubt was by its projectors intended to do, it became another means of drawing them away. If these branches while they lasted did not tend much to increase the population, they acted as a check upon emigration and very much increased the trade at the store, and about this time it came into the hands of Potter and Rice. Mr. Potter was young and *intensely active*, and desirous of increasing the business at *least* up to the demands of the times.

The leading citizens, among whom was the minister and some of the most prominent members of the church, fully appreciating the activity and enterprise of their young merchant, but not altogether approving his methods nor the direction things had taken in the store and tavern, then connected and carried on under the same management, and as a desire or at least a willingness on the part of Mr. Rice to sell out his interest became known, they conceived the idea of placing Deacon Allen in a more central position, where his ability as an accountant or book-keeper would find ample scope, as well as bring him within easier reach of those who needed his services as magistrate or in other ways. And another and the more *important* consideration with them was that with his well known conservatism and carefulness, his sterling integrity and Christian character, united with the business enthusiasm and supposed ability of Mr. Potter, he might serve as a *counterpoise*, and a safer and better state of things *morally* as well as in the line of business might thereby be secured.

These were the days of almost unlimited *credit* in the purchase and sale of store goods and farm products. The merchant having established his standing in city and country, could buy *ad libitum*, and could if so disposed increase his sales to almost

3

an unlimited extent so long as no equivalent was required except charges upon his books. If those who had little or no pecuniary resources did not dress well and fare sumptuously every day, it must have been because of their inherent objection to purchasing what they knew they could not pay for. Whether Mr. Rice, who was a farmer, saw the drift towards bankruptcy in the manner in which the business in Oakham as well as in other towns (North Brookfield by no means excepted) is not known, but for reasons satisfactory to himself he proposed to sell out. At the time the books of the firm showed some forty or fifty thousand dollars of accounts receivable (?) and a lesser but large amount of indebtedness. Mr. Rice proposed to transfer his entire interest and responsibility to the new firm of Potter and Allen. The stock of goods, fixtures and accounts were to be appraised by two disinterested men. In the appraisal of the accounts due the old firm large deductions were made. Those which were considered *worthless* were thrown out, and upon such as were denominated *doubtful* various discounts were made, but those which were called *good* went into the invoice at their full amount. From the total the (then known) payables being deducted, the balance was found against the new firm. Deacon Allen sold his farm and stock and put in all the proceeds, and took his place at the desk as the accountant. But he soon found by the coming in of claims for produce for which no credit had been given on the books on the one hand, and the impossibility of making collections to anything like the amount indicated by the invoice on the other hand, that he had bought a *stranded ship* which must soon go to pieces by the action of the waves. The final crash did not come till just after a new store building had been completed and occupied in the fall of 1836. Within a few months after his taking possession Deacon Allen told the writer that he was financially ruined and could do nothing but await inevitable failure, as the state of the business was entirely beyond his control. He of course was sorry to lose the earnings and savings of his previous lifetime, but what saddened him most was that he must occupy the position of a *bankrupt*. While under this strain of anxiety and suspense he was so far as possible the same cheerful Christian man in his family, in the church and Sunday School and in the town as before ; endeavoring all the while to fortify himself and prepare his family for approaching changes. His Christian duty seemed to him to be *submission* to what he regarded as a trying dispensation of Divine Providence. He was never known to cast any severe reflections upon those by whom consciously or unconsciously he had been victimized. He stayed by till the spring of 1837 (about six months after the failure) and did what he could to settle an unsettleable bankrupt estate, and than again betook himself to farming on a very limited scale, beginning with a single acre and adding thereto from time to time as he was able to purchase by his earnings as land surveyor and other employments, to which a sympathizing and friendly public called him; and thus by unceasing industry, economy and self denial on his part and that of his family, he afterwards became the owner of a comfortable home, proving himself to be the same cheerful and godly man in his worn and faded garments, and his old-time long woollen frock, that he had been in more affluent circumstances.

Those farmers who were heavy losers by the failure never felt like reproaching him, as they did not see that he was at all to be blamed, but they rather regarded him with pity and sorrow, as having been the *greatest sufferer*.

It may appear to the reader *very strange* that Deacon Allen and his advisers should have been so deceived that he should become a party to such a transaction as the purchase of an interest in a business which was then upon the border of ruin. The worst abuses of the credit system (concerning which very little could ever be said favorably), had for years been gradually creeping into the business of the community, so that no man at that time even *thought* of trying to do any kind of business to any considerable extent upon any other basis. The credit *folly* was neither local nor exceptional, but universal throughout the entire country, and business men generally seemed to be totally oblivious of a coming crisis, which, if the laws of trade mean anything, was *sure* to follow: the only question being that of time. The culmination was the great crash all over the country of 1837. In this particular case no living man, not even the proprietors themselves, had any reasonable *knowledge* or any *just conception* of the true condition of their business at the time that the firm name was changed to Potter and Allen.

Deacon Allen's life-long motto for *himself*, as well as for others, had been to "follow the leadings of Providence," and there can be no doubt that when he left the old farm and went into the store he verily believed that he was so doing, nor that the step was taken after prayerful consideration. And who shall presume to decide that he was mistaken? That he *needed* such an experience for his own good or discipline would be far from the thought of any one who knew the *man*. That question must be classed with things unknowable. One thing at least seems to be apparent: if he had never experienced a trial like this, neither he nor the world could ever have known how well he could bear such a test of his Christian character. Nobody can know what his after life would have been had he never been called to pass through this trial; how much it ministered to his Christian humility; his carefulness; his clearing himself from worldly entanglements; his more vehement desire to give himself to Christian service, rendering it *possible* that he thereafter might have lived less for *time* and more for *eternity*, and been a better man when he came to the close of life than he otherwise might have been. When we consider how slight a change from a man's plans or expectations may hinder his embarkation upon a doomed steamer or carry him into a railroad disaster, or change the whole current of his after life for better or worse, we see the utter folly of human speculations upon the orderings of Divine Providence. This happened to him when he was about five years past the middle of his earthly life, while he was still physically and mentally strong. Such reverses of fortune to human vision appear at any time of life to be deplorable, and the more so when they occur to one later in life, after his ability to labor for the restoration of lost fortune has become small and still growing less; that the fruits of many years of toil, upon which one in life's decline must needs begin to rely for sustenance, should be ruthlessly swept away by fire or flood or other cause, and actual *poverty* ensue; the case seems even more dark and discouraging. But the very fact itself so enlists the sympathy of relatives and friends towards one who has led an industrious and useful life, that neither he nor his can be left to suffer actual *want* in a Christian or in an appreciative community; and thus what seems only like *loss* may even become moral or spiritual gain to one who is properly exercised thereby.

Though at the time of his decease Deacon Allen might have been poorer in worldly estate, he may for aught we know have been richer in faith and heir to a richer inheritance in the life to come. This single event is dwelt upon so much at length because of its apparent importance and magnitude, because of the sudden transition of the whole family from a condition of comparative affluence to one of poverty at a time not much preceding the failing health, the *severe* sickness and the resultant death of Mrs. Allen, and because of the great change it (seemingly) must have made in his future and that of his family.

AS A CIVIL ENGINEER OR LAND SURVEYOR.

These employments tended to make him a good pedestrian. Being of full manly stature (six feet in height), active in every limb and muscle, and having frequent calls to leave his field or other home work and shoulder his instruments and do jobs of surveying in the town or in neighboring towns, he seldom travelled to such engagements by team, which in many cases would have been a hindrance rather than a help, and thus he became inured to foot travel. If his job was five or even ten miles away the same rule was generally observed. Being a rapid walker, and knowing full well that the shortest way between two points was a straight line, he discarded circuitous and crooked roads and found his way across fields and pastures, along hillsides or the borders of swamps; and thus he could many times save time as well as expense by going on foot. He was never late in meeting his appointments because he started off in season, and he started in due time, because by early rising he had time to prepare. If he went forth for a day's work and by diligence accomplished his task and reached home before night, he adapted his dress and did an hour's needed work in the garden or elsewhere before night-fall, had just time for supper and a brief visit with his wife and children, and was then ready to meet an evening appointment from which he promptly returned. Such was his command and economy of time that he never did anything in undue haste, nor wasted a moment in delay after his work was done. He always had just time enough for every duty and his work was so systematized that each engagement received due and timely attention. He never postponed till to-morrow that which could be done to-day.

His records and accounts were so kept that had he been
stricken down at any moment his work could readily have been
taken up where he left off. His plans and doings were all
apparent to the persons especially interested in them. About
the time when he was to leave the mercantile *wreck* in 1837
there came to him from an entire stranger of New York city a
proposition to employ him for several months as surveyor of a
large tract of wild land in the State of Maine, for which service
he was offered such compensation as he might himself see fit to
demand. His reply brought a visit from this stranger which
resulted in an engagement of about three months in the Maine
forest, for which his sound bodily health and ready adaptation
to a life in the woods especially fitted him, and at the same time
afforded him an opportunity to replenish his depleted personal
treasury, as well as a removal for a time from his unpleasant
surroundings at home. He never knew but little of the plans or
successes of this "Speculator in Eastern Lands," whose name
was Niels Brock Gram. The surveyor used to tell of his good
appetite and pleasant experiences as well as his arduous labors
in the Maine woods. When the first Sabbath morning dawned
upon him and his men, they remarked to him that they supposed
they were to work that day, but he said *no*, as he was not
accustomed to work upon the Sabbath day. He had with him
his Bible and other suitable reading, and the day was filled up
by their perusal and appropriate religious conversation with his
helpers, who never afterwards mentioned working upon the
Sabbath.

After this, calls in the line of surveying or engineering
became more frequent and remunerative than ever before. In
1857 he was elected as one of the Commissioners for Worcester
County and was the engineer of the Board during his service of
three years, and was beloved as well as respected by his associates in that office.

IN HIS FAMILY AND HOME.

The earlier home is more especially referred to because better
known to the writter. It was characterized by industry, frugality, harmony and happiness. In the management of the children
there was perfect concord between the parents. The children
were obedient and happy. There was absolute government in

the home circle and never a doubt as to where authority resided. Corporal punishment for transgression was unnecessary. If the child did that which was right it was sure to receive the approval of parents; if for any reason it had failed in any particular, gentle words of reproof or a look of disapproval was all that was needed: there was no place for pains or penalties in the family system. His ideas of family government are well expressed by a celebrated English writer: "In order to establish complete authority and secure obedience, the following rule must be invariably acted upon.—that *no command, either by word, look or gesture,* should be given which *is not intended to be enforced and obeyed.* It is the rock on which most parents split in infantile education, that while they are almost incessantly giving commands to their children, they are not careful to see that they are punctually obeyed, and seem to consider occasional violations of their injunctions as a very trivial fault, or as a matter of course. There is no practice more common than this, and none more ruinous to the authority of parents, and to the best interests of their offspring. When a child is accustomed by frequent repetitions to counteract the will of his parents, a habit of insubordination is gradually induced, which sometimes grows to such a height that neither entreaties nor threats, nor corporal punishment are sufficient to counteract its tendencies; and a sure foundation is laid for many future perplexities and sorrows. The rule, therefore, should be absolute,—that every paternal command be reasonable, that a compliance with it produce no *unnecessary* pain or trouble to the child; that it be expressed in words of *kindness* and *affection;* that it ought never to be delivered in a spirit of *passion* or *resentment.* Reproof or correction given in a rage, and with words of fury, is always considered as the effect of weakness and a want of self command, and uniformly frustrates the purpose it was intended to subserve."

While living on the farm he was frequently away from home during some part of the day. About the time of his expected return the little children were watching, and when they descried his well known figure in the distance they began the race to meet him. The one who could travel fastest would first gain his hand, and so on till the smallest who had scarcely toddled across the broad door-yard would be the last to be gathered in. He had a kindly greeting for each and fingers enough for all to take hold upon. They were asked if they had been happy to-day and the like, and would all assist in leading him into the house.

In 1836, when Emily was barely able to creep, the writer chanced to call upon Deacon Allen in the store, and was invited to go to the house for supper before his return to his place of labor in Smithville, Barre. Mrs. Allen put the baby down upon the floor that she might prepare the meal, but the child not appreciating the necessity of its temporary separation from its mother, followed her into the pantry pleading to be restored to her arms, whereupon she asked the father if he would take charge of her while she could set the table. He took her up, but that was not what the child just then wanted; her spunk arose and she became too straight and rigid to accommodate herself to the paternal lap, and attempted to slide down upon the floor. With his hands placed firmly upon each side her arms were pinioned and he raised her up and brought her into a sitting posture upon his right knee, and closing in his left knee, she found herself bound hand and foot, and heard a gentle but firm voice saying, "*Emma, sit still, sit still.*" She struggled for a moment, but in vain, and soon broke down and fell back upon her father's breast sobbing and grieving as if her little heart was broken. But it was not the heart but the *will* which had given way. She soon became quiet and the tea was served as if nothing had happened. After a while the father remarked to the visitor that the first lesson children need to learn is *submission*, and they cannot learn it too young: that this child had never resisted his will before, and that she would never do it again; that the work was done and the question of authority in the child's mind was settled forever. At another time at the table an older daughter was relating what had just taken place in the singing-school. She told what a certain other young lady said or did, and what followed from the teacher, closing with the remark that it was generally understood by the other scholars that she was virtually *turned out of school.* After hearing her through her father said, "I do not quite like *that* expression." The daughter blushed, and modified her opinion somewhat, putting a more charitable construction upon the pupil's behavior and divesting her story of some of its severity; "that's better," was all that was needed to restore harmony of opinions upon that subject. That there was family government in the household, no one who chanced to be there could doubt, nor that it was a government of *law*, and that that law was the law of *love*.

AS A TRUSTEE.

Having been a pupil at the Leicester Academy, and well and favorably known there, he was in August, 1834, chosen one of its Trustees, which office he held till 1852, and much enjoyed his annual attendance upon the examinations and the renewal of acquaintances. It is related of him that while he was in office the Trustees were called together in relation to an important case of discipline. In after conversation the Principal asked him what he would do in certain supposed cases which called for discipline. His brief but comprehensive reply was, "If I had a case of discipline on my hands I should never *adjourn* it."

AS A PUBLIC OFFICIAL.

For any public office he was never a self-appointed candidate. When chosen to office in town, county or State it was because a majority of his constituents preferred him to any other candidate. Records show that he was Moderator of the annual town meeting at four different times; Fence Viewer three years; Highway Surveyor four years; Selectman six years; Collector and Constable one year; Assessor nine years; Overseer of Poor one year; School Committee thirty-two years; Town Clerk eighteen years. As recording officer his *records* bear ample testimony to his efficiency, by the elegance of his penmanship and the concise and careful manner in which his work was done. He was County Commissioner for three years; a member of the House of Representatives in 1833, 1834, 1838 and 1858, four years; of the State Senate in 1839, 1841 and 1842, three years.

He was first commissioned a Justice of the Peace January 12, 1820, and held the office till his decease. He gave considerable attention to the study of law. Though never admitted to the Bar he was legal authority for his town and acted as its magistrate for many years.

As to his special services as a member of the Legislature we have but little data, except what the records at the State House show of his committee service. During his first year in the House he was not on any committee. In 1834 on Education; 1838 on Roads and Bridges; in 1858 on Agriculture (House Chairman); in the Senate in 1839 on Mercantile Affairs and Insurance; in 1841 on Parishes and Religious Societies; in 1812 on Parishes and Religious Societies (Chairman). In those years under *town* representation there was a much *larger* number of members than now, while the number of committees was *less*, so that there was a large proportion of the members who did not have places on any committees.

In 1841, a young man who was reared in Oakham under the instruction and influence of Deacon Allen called upon him in the Senate chamber (in recess time), and held a pleasant conversation, during which he spoke of his agreeable experiences in that body. The young man under a feeling of discouragement in relation to himself said, " I am glad of your own promotion and pleasant duties and associations, but one whose opportunities for an education were as limited as mine have been can never expect to be thus promoted and honored." To which he responded, " Don't be discouraged; a man's chances for promotion to public service or honor depend far less upon his school education, over which he had no control, than they do upon a good character, the formation of which is entirely in his own hands." According to his custom, some illustrative story must be told, and he proceeded to say that a few days ago a fellow-member approached him in a cautious and confidential manner and said, " Deacon Allen, will you please tell me the meaning of the Latin Mr. ——— made use of in his speech?" I replied that " It would give me pleasure to be able do so, but, my dear sir, I don't know a word of Latin myself." So the gentleman found he was not alone in not having been favored with a collegiate education.

It is not presumed that he gained his good standing in the legislature by long, or learned, or eloquent speeches, but by being able as a common-sense man to express himself clearly and handsomely, so that he was by no means looked down upon as an inferior, but respected as a peer among his fellows. He was also, no doubt, faithful and efficient in committee work.

As he always enjoyed good society, his winters in the Senate were a great pleasure to him. One term his seat was next to that of Josiah Quincy, to whose house he was often invited, as well as to the mansion of Gov. Edward Everett. He often met Lowell Mason and Jacob Abbott, and boarded at the same hotel with Samuel Williston and Henry Wilson.

He made but few speeches in the Legislature, because of the diffidence he felt about speaking before the noted and scholarly men by whom he was surrounded; but at home, in Oakham, before any audience, he spoke freely and well.

IN THE CHURCH AND SABBATH SCHOOL.

His Christian life began about the time of his first marriage, in 1817. He joined the church the same year. Within a few years from this time nearly one hundred and fifty persons were added to the church.

Having decided to live a *Christian life*, he, without delay, called his household together (including the hired men); told them of the step he had taken, erected the "*family altar*," and entered at once upon the service of his Master with unflinching zeal and earnestness.

He was chosen a deacon of the church in Oakham in November, 1817, and held that office at the time of his death, in 1870, about fifty-three years, and was immediately succeeded by his only son, Jesse Allen. He always sustained and cheerfully co-operated with his minister, working with him so far as he possibly could do, and was never identified with those who for any unimportant reason sought a change. He was careful and anxious to prevent any dissensions between the members of the church, or variance between himself and his brethren.

On Thursday afternoon immediately preceding Communion Sabbath, it was the custom of the church to assemble and listen to the "Preparatory Lecture" by the pastor. While teaching the school, in 1834, before alluded to, one of these occasions occurred. As the church bell began to toll, he said to the school that he desired to attend, that he would appoint a certain scholar to take his place for the time being, and also invite any and all in the school who were members of the church to accompany him. Several accepted, and on the way he expressed his pleasure that they had done so, and advised them to make it their rule to attend these meetings, remarking as we walked from the school-house to the sanctuary, that he had come to regard the duty and privilege of such attendance as an obligation second only to the duty of attending public worship on the Sabbath.

When he became a member of the church, the *Sunday School* work was in its infancy. Aided by Mr. Stephen Lincoln, he visited the people from house to house, inviting the children to come together upon an appointed Sabbath, when the school was first organized in Oakham, in 1818, he being chosen Superintendent, which position he held, with one or two years exception, till 1860 (a period of forty years), when he was succeeded by Deacon James Packard. Mr. Stephen Lincoln was the first Assistant Superintendent, and for more than half a century these two co-laborers were permitted to give their earnest and successful efforts in this department, in the service of the One they loved so well. The school at one time numbered more than three hundred members. Colonel John Robinson, Deacon Andrew Spooner, Deacon William Spooner, Deacon Solomon Crocker and several others were very efficient aids in this work. Oakham, in the days of these men, as well as ever since, has borne the reputation of having one of the largest Sabbath schools in proportion to its Sabbath audiences in the vicinity.

Deacon Allen was not a theologian in the generally accepted sense of the term. Brought up by pious parents, and early instructed in the Bible and Assembly's Catechism, which was held in great veneration by the Christian fathers and mothers, taught not only in their families, but as was required by the law of the State, in the public schools for many years after he became a school teacher. He regarded the expressions of divine truth therein contained as essential elements in a Christian education of children, and so he and his excellent wives taught it to their children. But in the discussions and disputations of these doctrines of the church, which were quite common, he was never known to take part. If such were thrust upon him, he had a ready faculty of turning the conversation upon some more agreeable and practical theme. Here he doubtless agreed with Dr. Thomas Dick, the English writer from whom we quote, who uses this language :—

" A disposition to introduce quibbling and useless metaphysical distinctions has been the bane of *theology*, and one of the causes of the divisions in the Christian church."

He was not much given to argument upon any subject, but ever ready to state his own convictions or conclusions upon any worthy question and there leave the matter for others to think of or discuss after he had withdrawn. In his counsels to young men, as to what plans of life they should make, or what pursuits follow, his advice might be reduced to these two propositions :—

First, be a Christian.

Second, follow the leadings of Providence.

In his view a successful and happy life does not so much depend upon the wisdom of a human plan of usefulness or greatness, as upon a conscientious discharge of each and every apparent duty in its time, and in the sphere in which the doer finds himself.

He was deeply interested in church music ; was himself a correct singer, and had a tolerable use of the violoncello, which he used for bass in family worship, himself singing tenor, the other parts being well sustained by the other members of the family. His own voice was *very light* for one of his size and robustness. The change of voice from its normal strength came upon him by a severe sickness in early life, but he could discourse sweet and agreeable music. The instrument above-mentioned he used for many years to carry to the church on Sundays, playing and singing in the church choir. He also appointed and conducted singing schools for the children of the Sabbath School.

HIS REPUTATION.

It is obviously true that every person *should* have accorded to him the reputation to which his character and conduct justly entitle him, but to such a rule there are many exceptions. Envy, jealousy or political competition or preference sometimes lead to the bestowal of undeserved commendation or to unjust censure upon public men. Party or local prejudices sometimes make their appearance in giving false coloring to what may be said for or against the candidate for office. Individual ambitions or aspirations have their influence in the formation of the public reputation of worthy citizens. To such and similar influences be never to any great extent seemed to be subjected. No man who valued his *own* reputation seemingly *dared* to reproach *him*. To his own prudence and unquestioned integrity and faithfulness in all the trusts imposed upon him, was in great measure no doubt due the fact that he as a rule escaped unjust censure or abuse. It seems little less than remarkable that a man who occupied so many positions of honor and service should have so little said against him by unscrupulous or irreligious men who were common fault-finders in regard to professed Christians in his day.

A minor son was once consulting his father in relation to his desire to unite himself with the church. His father expressed his own sorrow and disappointment that his son should choose to identify himself with that class of people, saying that he had better hopes concerning his future standing in the community; that if he would be in favor and honor in the town he must associate himself with a different class, illustrating his view of the matter by mentioning several honored names in the town who did not belong to the church. The son replied by asking his father "What objection have you to my being associated with such men as Deacon Allen?" The father replied hastily and with considerable warmth, "I wasn't talking about Deacon Allen, I meant such men as Mr. ———, and Mr. ———, and others." Very few seemed to have anything to say against Deacon Allen concerning any of his words or actions; and thus he was permitted to enjoy "A good name which is rather to be chosen than great riches, and loving favor rather than silver and gold."

Deacon Allen's Christian life and labors occurred at a period of time when those who were regarded as *very pious* people, or the *best* type of Christians, were as a rule very solemn and sober minded, so much so that a lively or even a cheerful demeanor was regarded as being inconsistent with a religious profession or a devout Christian life and character. Sober mindedness in its most literal sense was an evidence of piety. The most serious and solemn phases of religion, such as accountability to God; the uncertainty of life; the dread event of death; the coming judgment and eternal retribution were dwelt upon in the services of the sanctuary and in the prayer meetings, and that Christian cheerfulness and happiness which properly belong to the child of redeeming grace, like that to which *he* was inclined, were kept in the background and seemed like *innovation* upon the prevailing sentiment He might properly be said to have lived and acted in a *transition* period of the church from the *solemn* and *sad* to the more *cheerful* view of human life and destiny. His character had not only its kindly and cheerful aspect but also its *sterner* side, without which he could not have been the commanding or influential personage that he was in the family, school, church, Sabbath school, the town meeting or elsewhere. Possessed of great will power, quick decision and abiding firmness, the look or facial expression which accompanied the *command* where he was in authority, or the needed *rebuke*, could only be interpreted or understood as meaning prompt *obedience* or *compliance*. He was *feared* as well as *loved*. To a few persons, especially to the young who were inclined to misbehave themselves, his austerity might have seemed to be a predominant trait, but to those who were his pupils, or were in condition to *know* him more fully, his kindliness was so manifest that *their* fear of him became only reverence, prompting them to a ready compliance with his wishes. He might be called a terror to evil doers, but he was emphatically a praise to those who did well.

It is not known that he ever joined a secret society. He was one of the *first* to become a total abstainer from all intoxicating beverages. In politics he was never a strong partisan. He acted with the Whig, and afterwards with the Republican parties. What Chauncey M. Depew said of George Washington, February 22, 1888, would as well apply to James Allen. " He was not so abnormally developed in any direction as to be called a genius, yet he was the strongest because the best balanced, the fullest rounded, the most even and self-masterful of men ; the incarnation of common sense and moral purity of action and repose." Another says, " The best Christian is simply the highest style of man." And still another, " Man's way to be great is by *ruling* others. God's way to be great is by *serving* others." Upon this latter proposition Deacon Allen seemed to have acted, and so when his life work was accomplished he was ready to die ; coming in from his labors as cheerfully as the tired servant obeys the call of his master to quit the field and come to the *rest* of the home at eventide.

The last time he was seen alive by the writer was about three weeks before his death. He was reclining upon his bed dressed in his usual clothing, indicating that he was still able to walk, and perhaps step out of the house. He seemed to be fully conscious that the end was rapidly drawing near. He was as calm and self-composed as if in perfect health. He spoke of his past life and labors, dwelling especially upon the religious influence he had felt bound by his official position in the church to exert, remarking that he hoped he had in some humble measure succeeded in fulfilling that sacred trust; that in looking backward he found very little to regret and very much to be thankful for; that his trust in God was *unshaken*, and that no fear or dread of bodily dissolution troubled him. Death came June 18, 1870.

His funeral was attended in the meeting-house on Monday, P. M., June 20, the services being conducted by his brother-in-law, Rev. Leonard S. Parker.

> Joy in heaven, songs of gladness,
>   Earth's battles fought, faith's victories won;
> On earth sorrow, though not sadness,
>   The *just*, the *good*, the *lov'd* has gone.

> " He may be great who proudly rears
>   For coming years strong pyramids;
>   But greater he who hourly builds
>   A character by noble deeds.

> " He may be wise whose mind is filled
>   With all the wisdom time has given;
>   Who sees and does his duty well
>   Is wiser in the sight of Heaven.

> " It may be great to deck the walls
>   With pictures by rare genius wrought;
>   Greater it is to line the soul
>   With tints and gems of noble thought.

> " He may be great who can indite
>   Songs that shall every bosom thrill;
>   He who knows how to make his life
>   A *Poem grand* is greater still."

—*Selected.*

"Were a star quenched on high,
    For ages would its light,
    Still travelling downward from the sky,
    Shine on our mortal sight.

"So when a great man dies,
    For ages beyond our ken,
    The light he leaves behind him lies
    Upon the paths of men."

—*Longfellow.*

4

GENEALOGICAL REGISTER.

ALLEN, Rev. SAMUEL (1), and his wife Ann, of Braintree (since Dorchester), came from England in 1632.

2. **Samuel**, son of Samuel 1, was *b.* in 1632, moved to East Bridgewater as early as 1660 : *m.* Sarah Partridge, of Duxbury. He was a deacon and town clerk.

3. **Nathaniel**, son of Samuel 2, was *b.* in 1672 ; *m.* Bethia Conant in 1696.

4. **James**, son of Nathaniel 3, was *b.* in 1704 ; *m.* Mary Packard in 1732.

5. **Jesse**, son of James 4, *b.* in 1744 ; *m.* Abigail, daughter of Dr. Stoughton Willis in 1768, and soon thereafter came to Oakham ; he *d.* April 11, 1816 ; she *d.* Sept. 20, 1829. Their children : OLIVE, *b.* Oct. 26, 1770 : *d.* ———, unmarried. PARNEL, *b.* Dec. 25, 1772 ; *m.* Timothy Nye, of Oakham. LUCINDA, *b.* Dec. 25, 1774 : *d.* at the age of 18 years. HANNAH, *b.* Feb. 7, 1777 ; *m.* Capt. Little, of New Braintree. CLOE, *b.* Aug. 10, 1779 : *m.* (1) Jonas Leonard, (2) Rev. Gaius Conant. ABIGAIL, *b.* July 12, 1784 : *m.* (1) Dr. Seth Fobes, of Oakham, (2) Rev. Mr. Gusha. LUCY, *b.* Jan. 6, 1788 ; *m.* Col. Henry Penniman, of New Braintree. JAMES, *b.* July 2, 1792 **6.**

6. **James**, son of Jesse 5, *m.* (1) Feb. 21, 1816, Polly L., daughter of Nathaniel Crocker, Esq., of Paxton, she *d.* July 5, 1841, aged 46 ; (2) Sept. 10, 1842, Hannah H. Parker, of Dunbarton, N. H., who *d.* May 22, 1881, aged nearly 73. He *d.* June 18, 1870, aged 78. Children by 1st wife : LOUISA, *b.* April 21, 1817 : *m.* June 19, 1838, Hiram Knight, of North Brookfield (formerly of Oakham) ; and *d.* Nov. 11, 1839. [Her child, James Allen Knight, *b.* Sept. 8, 1839, *m.* Sept. 22, 1862, Susan M. Swift, of Southbridge, and *d.* Aug. 10, 1863, on board of steamer *Granite State* on Long Island Sound, on his way home from New Orleans, where he had served as a private

in Company F, 42d Regiment, M. V. M.] STOUGHTON WILLIS, *b.* June 6, 1820; *d.* March 17, 1834. JAMES, *b.* July 4, 1822; *d.* March 22, 1830. ABIGAIL, *b.* May 30, 1825; *m.* March 26, 1846. Samuel B. Fairbank, of Oakham. Soon thereafter they were sent as missionaries by the A. B. C. F. M. to Ahmednugger, India; she *d.* at Bombay, Aug. 21, 1852. [Their children: Emily Maria Fairbank, *b.* Nov. 21, 1846. Mary Crocker, *b.* and *d.* in Nov., 1849. John Mellen, *b.* Aug. 8, 1852; *d.* Nov., 1854. Their daughter Emily Maria, *m.* March 21, 1871, Thomas Snell Smith, in Concord, Ill. Their children: Mary Fairbank (Smith), *b.* Jan. 19, 1872. Emily Maria, *b.* July 10, 1874. Tirzah Snell, *b.* March 13, 1879. Abby Allen, *b.* Aug. 29, 1882. Allen Fairbank, *b.* May 30, 1884. Thomas Herbert, *b.* May 15, 1885.] MARY L., *b.* Sept. 1, 1827; *m.* June 17, 1849, William Lincoln, of Oakham; and *d.* there June 7, 1851. [An infant child was buried with its mother.] GEORGE, *b.* April 3, 1829; *d.* Sept. 24, 1829. LUCY, *b.* Feb. 27, 1830; *m.* (1) Rev. Joseph Dexter Poland, of North Brookfield, who *d.* Aug. 1, 1853; (2) April 1, 1857, Nathaniel Spear; and *d.* March 10, 1861. He *d.* Feb. 26, 1867, aged 40. [Their children: William Dexter (Spear), *b.* Feb. 15, 1859. Allen Crocker, *b.* Feb. 21, 1861.] MARIA, *b.* June 21, 1832; *m.* June 23, 1852, William Lincoln, of Oakham, and *d.* May 22, 1855. He *d.* Dec. 1, 1856. [Their child: Mary E. Lincoln, *b.* July 18, 1853; *m.* Prof. George I. Alden, of the Worcester Polytechnic Institute; *d.* Nov. 12, 1876. Their children: Clara Louise (Alden), *b.* April 26, 1873. Mary Frances, *b.* May 1, 1876; *d.* Jan. 6, 1879.] EMILY KIMBALL, *b.* Sept. 15, 1835; *d.* Aug. 26, 1845. Children by 2d wife: LOUISA PARKER, *b.* July 12, 1843; *m.* Dec. 14, 1870, Hon. Sanford B. Kellogg, of St. Louis, Mo. [Their children: Alice Welch (Kellogg), *b.* Nov. 14, 1871. George Dwight, *b.* June 28, 1873.] HANNAH MERRIAM, *b.* May 9, 1845; *d.* May 16, 1863, aged 18. She was a young lady greatly beloved by all who knew her; a very fine singer; a teacher in the public schools, and had the charge of the infant department in the Sabbath School two or three years previous to her death. At her funeral her pastor, Rev. F. N. Peloubet, spoke of her as the sweet "singer of Israel." JESSE, *b.* May 23, 1847; *m.* Dec. 28, 1881, Lizzie Sumner, of Hebron, Ct. [Their children: James (Allen), *b.* in Oakham, Nov. 7, 1882; Alice Buel, *b.* Oct. 13, 1883. Eva Sumner, *b.* May 17, 1888.] MARTHA BIRD, *b.* April 7, 1849.

CROCKER, NATHANIEL, son of Job and Mary, *b.* June 30, 1758; *m.* Mehitable Lewis, who was *b.* July 1, 1762, and *d.* Jan. 31, 1835, aged 73, and was buried near Ware's Corners (so called) in Oakham. He *d.* at Buffalo, N. Y., with his son

George L., in August, 1855, lacking only two years and ten months of being a centenarian. Their children: Job, *b.* Aug. 28, 1784; *d.* July 6, 1814. George, *b.* July 27, 1786; *d.* July 6, 1793. Nathaniel, *b.* March 30, 1788; settled in Dixmont, Me., had a large family, and *d.* about 1873. Robert, *b.* July 18, 1790; *d.* Nov. 2, 1800. Solomon (Dea.), *b.* June 23, 1792; *m.* Dec. 4, 1817, Abigail Warren; and *d.* in Oakham, April 13, 1855, buried at Ware's Corners. They settled in Royalston and lived there till failing health compelled a change of business, and he bought the farm in Oakham, afterwards owned by the late Thatcher A. Morgan, lived upon it a little over a year, and *d.* as above, leaving five young children then living. The entire family were as follows: Abigail Warren, *b.* Jan. 9, 1820; *m.* Charles W. Smith (had five children of whom four are now living); and *d.* March 14, 1859, aged 39. Reliance, *b.* Oct. 20, 1821; *m.* Edward Kendall. Mary Lewis, *b.* Aug. 15, 1827. William Warren, *b.* Nov. 7, 1823; *d.* May 17, 1830. Nathaniel Lewis, *b.* Feb. 6, 1826; *d.* April 10, 1826. Caroline, *b.* Aug. 2, 1830. Solomon, *b.* March 8, 1835; *d.* March 1, 1840. "The dear little son (Solomon) who was baptized at the bed-side of his dying father who consecrated him to God, hoping he might live to be a missionary, was permitted to live until he was nearly five years of age when it pleased our Heavenly Father to take him home. How hard it was to give him up, our only brother; he was a beautiful child, so sweet, too good for earth." The wife and mother who lived with her daughter, Mrs. Kendall, the last twenty years of her life, died at the age of 83 years and 11 months. Polly L., *b.* Nov. 18, 1794; *m.* Feb. 21, 1816, James Allen, of Oakham 6; and *d.* July 5, 1841. George Lewis, probably *b.* about 1797; had a large family; lived in Albany and Buffalo, N. Y. Meritable, *b.* Dec. 6, 1801; *d.* unmarried. Abigail L., *b.* Oct. 17, 1804; *m.* (1) Mr. Bursley by whom she had a son Samuel; (2) Mr. Adams of Northbridge. Reliance, *b.* April 30, 1807; *m.* John S. Mellen; and *d.* in Albany, N. Y.

PARKER, WILLIAM (Capt.), the eldest son of William and Hannah (Hardy), came from puritan ancestry, residing for several generations in Essex Co., Mass. He was a native of Wenham in said county, *b.* Jan. 9, 1773; *m.* (1) April 7, 1796, Anna Stickney, of Bradford: (2) April 4, 1798, Martha Tenney, who was *b.* in Bradford, June 11, 1771: and *d.* Dec. 29, 1842. He *d.* Aug. 29, 1815. They removed to Dunbarton, N. H. Children: Ann, *b.* in Bradford, Jan. 18, 1799; *m.* Nov. 19, 1823, Rev. Isaac Bird, and they went out as missionaries. Emily, *b.* in Bradford, Sept. 5, 1800; *m.* Jan. 19, 1825, Rev.

James Kimball, who was for many years the minister in Oakham. He d. March 16, 1861; she d. Oct. 18, 1874. [Their children: Martha Ann, b. Nov. 10, 1825; d. Nov. 25, 1827. James Parker (Rev.), b. Dec. 29, 1828; m. (1) July 29, 1858, Mary B. Dickinson, of Rowley, who d. Jan. 10, 1873; (2) April 15, 1874, Jeannie King, of Suffield, Ct. He d. May 2, 1882, [Children of Rev. James P. and Mary B. Kimball: Mary Emily, b. in Granby, March 18, 1860; m. Sept., 1886, Rev. Geo. H. Cummings, once a teacher of North Brookfield High School; settled in Thompson, Ct. James Dickinson, b. in Falmouth, Dec. 27, 1861. William Sanford, b. Sept. 30, 1863; m. Aug., 1887, Abigail, dau. of President Stockbridge of Amherst; they reside in Foxboro, Mass. Julia Frances, b. in Foxboro, Nov. 19, 1865. Daniel Parker, b. in Foxboro, Dec. 3, 1867. Richard Lincoln, b. in Haydenville, Nov. 10, 1870; d. April 10, 1871. Caroline Louise, b. in Haydenville, Nov. 28, 1872.] Maria Louise, dau. of Rev. James and Emily Kimball, b. in Dunbarton, N. H., Aug. 2, 1830; m. Aug. 2, 1855, Sanford B. Kellogg, of St. Louis, Mo.; and d. Nov. 11, 1869. Their only child, Clara Louise Kellogg, was b. in Oakham, June 22, 1856; and m. in 1885, Rev. Marcus Taft, a missionary in China. They have a dau. Emily Louise, b. in 1887. William Bird, 2d son of Rev. James and Emily Kimball, b. in Oakham, June 2, 1833; m. Feb. 17, 1858, Fanny C. Woods, of Enfield, where they reside (no children). Daniel Tenney, their 3d son, b. in Oakham, July 24, 1835; d. April 16, 1864. Leonard Dascomb, their 4th son, b. in Oakham, Aug. 5, 1837; d. Aug. 26, 1837. WILLIAM, b. in Bradford, Sept. 8, 1802; m. April 14, 1834, Dolly Blake, of Exeter, N. H.; and d. April 23, 1865, in Winchester, Ill. MARTHA, b. Jan. 23, 1804; m. April 23, 1827, Rev. Thomas Tenney, of Chester, N. H. DAVID H. (Dea.), b. in Dunbarton, N. H., Jan. 9, 1807; m. (1) Nov. 7, 1833, Louisa Mills, of Dunbarton, who d. Nov. 27, 1841; (2) Dec. 8, 1842, Nancy Bassett, of Lee, Mass. [His children by 1st wife: Sarah M., b. Sept. 29, 1834. Mary Ann, b. Aug. 25, 1836; d. Dec. 10, 1872. Louisa, b. March 17, 1840. By 2d wife: Abby Jane, b. Sept. 21, 1846.] HANNAH H., b. in Dunbarton, N. H., Aug. 2, 1808; m. Sept. 10, 1842, Dea. James Allen 6, of Oakham; and d. there May 22, 1881. MARIANNE, b. in Dunbarton, July 1, 1810; m. April 14, 1834, Prof. James Dascomb; and d. Nov. 12, 1882. LEONARD STICKNEY, b. Dec. 6, 1812; m. (1) Sept. 20, 1838, Caroline A. Goodale, of Oakham, who d. Sept. 10, 1842; (2) Oct. 28, 1845, Mrs. Abigail Blake French. [Their children: Leonard Goodale, b. Aug. 2, 1839; m. May 1, 1863, Flavia Benton (they have nine children, and reside in Mason City, Ia.; he is a deacon and a farmer). Caroline Augusta, b. Nov. 27, 1840; m. Oct. 7, 1868, George S. Chase, and has had two children; resides in

Cambridge. **Mary Cornelia,** *b.* June 30, 1842; after her mother's death she was adopted by her Aunt Dascomb, and is now a missionary in Brazil; unm. **Abbie Blake,** *b.* Oct. 14, 1846: *m.* Nov. 7, 1872, Francis A. Fiske, of Concord, N. H., and has two children. **Henry French,** *b.* July 31, 1848; *d.* March 5, 1850. **Mary Lilian,** *b.* May 6, 1854; and lives with her parents in Cambridge, Mass.

DEACON ALLEN'S PICTURE.

Of the two likenesses of Mr. Allen now to be found, one is a double daguerreotype (of him and his second wife), extending downwards only to the waist; taken when he was about sixty-two years old. The likeness is a good one, showing him more as he used to appear when in earlier life he always had a smooth-shaven and plump face, his only neck-dress being a faultlessly white cravat or neck-cloth, without bow or knot or visible fastening. In this picture he retains much of his original comeliness of face and features, looking upon which carries one who knew him in his earlier prime back to the personal beauty or comeliness with which in face and form and manly stature he was by nature crowned.

The other likeness, which for reasons has been adopted, is a photograph taken about twelve or thirteen years later, and more readily recalls him as he appeared in later life. Could a likeness of him as he appeared in early manhood and as he is remembered by elderly people have been obtained, it would have been a valuable addition to this work. It is but just and true to say of him that he was not only one of the most able, active and influential men ever born in Oakham, but in personnel one of the most comely of her sons. For personal beauty when a boy, his aptness and proficiency in acquiring and performing, he was not only greatly doted upon by his parents, but *praised* by all, insomuch that he used to say that it was a wonder to himself that he had not been *spoiled* by excessive commendation and adulation.

In March, 1888, a circular letter was issued expressing an intention of writing a Life History of Deacon James Allen, and asking recipients to express themselves, in writing, upon such phases of his life and character as especially impressed the writers, giving what they knew by personal contact with him, or any knowledge they might possess which could be interwoven into the narrative ;—" or, *better still*, to arrange whatever they had to say, in such form that it could be inserted over their own names."

From several persons replies were received expressive of their interest in the proposed work, and their appreciation of Deacon Allen's character and labors, but modestly declining to contribute articles to be published, lest they might fail to express themselves adequately. No doubt their own *diffidence*, rather than lack of *ability*, was the chief obstacle in their way, and must account for the absence of a number of able articles upon the subject. But thanks to the writers, the following contributions have been received, and are published herewith as personal tributes to the memory of the man from whom so much of good influence has been derived, by these, as well as by other sons and daughters of Oakham. And not a little is added to the value of these contributions by their being so generally corroborative of each other, as well as of the work of the author.

TESTIMONIALS.

Enfield, Mass., March 30, 1888.

Among the earliest recollections of my boyhood days were the form and features of Deacon James Allen.

Large in stature, very erect, with an independent step—I had almost said stride, he moved along the street or the aisle in church, just as though he had an ownership in the land he walked on, and very important business to transact in the house of God. He was a grave man, increasingly so, no doubt, as the added years and trials weighed upon him. He was not given to much notice of children, as I remember, but I have not forgotten that he *once* commended me for industry, and the determination which I seemed to exhibit in overcoming one of the immense wood-piles of those early days. Very early I learned that he had a way of brightening up when a good story was told, and he was not far behind in the telling.

The misfortunes which overtook him were spoken of in the parsonage, and whenever an example of courage and fortitude under trial was needed, Deacon Allen was often referred to.

It has occurred to me in years past, and I desire to put it upon record, that the example which he set, the life which he lived, the teachings which he gave, in short, the character which he *was*, led many a young man to shoulder a musket, and to do what he could for the country which needed his assistance. Deacon Allen was brave and true, he was faithful as a friend; and here, as the only living representative of the family which for so many years occupied the parsonage, while he was in his prime, let me say that no pastor ever had a friend more firm and consistent, more helpful in time of trial, more bold to face opposition. He was the pastor's friend in very truth. Sometimes there was a lack of patience, occasionally a hasty word. He was stern and unyielding when occasion demanded,— not exactly sympathetic in his nature. He occupied many positions of trust and honor, and had several titles; more than once have I heard him say that he regarded the title of Deacon as most honorable of all, and this is the key to the intimacy with his pastor, and to the service which he gladly rendered to the church which honored him. This I regard as his leading trait—his interest in, and devotion to the church in Oakham.

He was very successful as a teacher. I was one of his pupils for several terms. He understood how to teach—to educate, and this he did many a time without regard to text-books. His experience helped. He had been, and was always a surveyor of land, and he was a careful observer, a surveyor of nature, critical, exact. He did not like lazy boys, and he was not always careful when laying his hands upon them. I am not sure that a teacher would be justified in these later times in pulling hair and pinching ears, as he sometimes did—I did not always escape, —but in looking back to the "East Centre School-house," and the days of long ago, I feel strongly drawn towards the teacher who did so much for me. His stories, told over and over, always had a point—any one of his scholars will remember about his losing his pencil-case from his right hand vest-pocket. How he recalled all the circumstances of an accident, how he remembered the exact position he took, and how he went and found the case just where he knew he lost it. He taught his pupils thus to be "particular to have a care for all their acts," and it would be of great value in the coming years. Another story must be recalled, and this illustrated the peculiar traits of the Chinese.

An American sea-captain was in one of the Chinese ports, and found that he needed some clothes (especially pantaloons, as our teacher stated). He took an old pair to the Chinese tailor, and told him to make the new garments *exactly* like the old. When he received them he found the tailor had done *exactly* as he told him, and had put in a neat little patch in the new goods, just where it was in the old. ("Our teacher" always smiled when this story was told). I think he was particularly attached to mathematics and excelled in arithmetic and algebra, but we were well posted in grammar, and could pick out the complicated sentences in Young and Pope.

I believe I am correct in saying that if there was any partiality shown when he was teacher, it was not in favor of the boys. Quite likely they needed something else more. I can see him now with his swinging step, coming down the long reach of road toward the school-house, thoughtful, grave, self-contained, at times severe, but all in all a teacher who was highly prized.

Deacon Allen was a capital moderator in town-meeting. He was never run over or abashed, but held the reins squarely and fairly. (The boys who sold molasses candy, and sometimes gingerbread, to the sovereigns for gain, were occasionally reminded in a public manner that they must be quiet or leave.) It was a pleasure to hear Moderator Allen call off the list of voters—as was his custom, when the polls were open. I question whether any assembly of citizens, in any town, was ever managed and handled, and kept in better order than were the town meetings of Oakham when Deacon James Allen was moderator. He was a careful, correct Town Clerk, a safe, judicious adviser, an official in town and county and State, whose record is of the best. He had an honorable ambition which was reasonably gratified. There did not seem to be any elation when he was promoted. His honors, so far as I can know and judge, came unsought and were in fact much more satisfactory and advantageous to the givers than to him. The people recognized his worth. In earlier years how much he did in a musical way! The old bass-viol was vigorously used, and the choir relied largely upon him, and what a help he was in the training of others, notably his own sweet-voiced family. Much might be said and written concerning his great love of his garden and its fruits,—for the orchards which he planted and renovated, and the knowledge he imparted to others in these directions.

He was authority in all these matters. But the years were passing, and he came to be an old man, and his varied, wearisome life work was done. He had seen much of trial and affliction. The much loved wife of his youth, the sons of his young manhood, the daughters, mature and useful, and one, the child of his later years, too rare a plant for bleak New England hills, all these had been taken from him. There remained to him the wife of his later years,—faithful and devoted, and children, able like their mother to cheer, comfort and care for him in his declining days. Like one of his famous apple-trees, though the years had been many and the seasons severe, though there had been drouth and loss of limb, yet carefully and tenderly nursed, a new growth had appeared, and precious fruit had clustered and ripened. His name and his fame are rich legacies to us all.

WILLIAM B. KIMBALL.

In a letter from Cambridge, Feb. 23, 1888, Rev. Leonard S. Parker, says :

" My acquaintance with Deacon Allen began more than fifty years ago. I went to Oakham to teach a select school of sixty pupils ; the first of the kind in the town. I well remember the warmth of his earliest greeting. The friendship then formed grew stronger with the lapse of years while his life lasted. His social qualities were very attractive. He was always self-poised and collected, ever ready to learn, and to impart to others what he knew. He was a great lover of the town in which he lived ; as a true citizen he sought to promote its highest prosperity, willing to perform any labor, to make any sacrifice for this end. He was specially interested in the subject of education. He had thought and read much upon the subject. When I first knew him he was a highly successful teacher. My eldest son was in his later years for a season under his instruction. His testimony was, that *he was the most thorough instructor he ever had.* Of one reason of this Deacon Allen once gave me an amusing account. In his school life he was accounted one of the most brilliant arithmeticians in town. His father, proud of his fame, once asked him to cast the interest on a note on which several payments had been made. 'I worked on it all day making the interest exceed the principal, and finally gave it up. Being deeply mortified, I went back to Simple Addition determined never to pass over any part of the book till I fully understood it.' What he had done he sought to make all his pupils do. As a Christian man Deacon Allen was one of the most consistent I ever knew. He was not carried away by any high excitement, but he was one you could count upon at all times. Not long after I entered the ministry I spent two weeks in Oakham, aiding the pastor in a season of special religious interest. Many of the young people whom he and I had taught were among the converts. It is pleasant to recall his looks and words and prayers at this time. Yet in earlier times of serious religious divisions in town and in seasons of less attention to the concerns of the soul, he was always serene and cheerful. He had a strong and abiding trust in the Living God. So under losses of property, and of kindred by death. He was the true friend and adviser of his pastor, and of all who needed counsel, —a model husband and father. I was with him for a time in his last sickness. We both knew that the end was near at hand. He spoke gratefully of his past, and humbly yet confidently of the eternal future. Thus lived and died the friend of my early and riper life, whom so many with me rise up and call him blessed, whose impress was and is for good on the town where he lived and wrought, whose memory is as ointment poured forth among all who have ever known him."

Rev. S. C. Dean, of South Bend, Nebraska, says in a letter of March 28, 1888 :—

My distinct recollection of Deacon James Allen, of Oakham, Mass., runs back for sixty years. He was superintendent of the Sunday School most of the time from its organization in 1818. For eighteen years, from 1828 to 1845, I was a constant attendant of the Oakham Sunday School under his superintendence. He taught day schools nearly every year from youth till old age. In many households parents, children and grandchildren went to school to him. I was a member of his school for three months. He was usually on the school committee and visited each year all the schools of the town. For two or three years he taught singing schools for little children.

He had been a member of the Massachusetts Legislature during the winters of 1831 and 1832 (?) and had become a great friend of Dr. Lowell Mason and others, who were the great Christian workers in the Boston Sunday Schools, especially in the musical department. When he came home in the summer of 1832 (?) he started a singing school for the Oakham children. I was one of the children at that time and attended his singing school that year and one or two succeeding years. He gave his time and labors for our good and the good of the Sunday School. He was a farmer at that time and lived a mile from town, but two afternoons in the week he would leave his work, haying, harvesting, or whatever it might be, to give instruction in music.

Sometimes he would come right from the harvest field in his work clothes, covered with perspiration. However pressing his work might be he would not disappoint the children. He was on hand at the appointed time. He loved the children and all the children in town knew it, and they loved him. He and a few other Christian workers have in the past done great things for Oakham and not for Oakham only, for hundreds of noble Christian men and women have gone forth from thence and are now scattered all over this land and some in foreign lands, most of them among the foremost Christian workers in the communities where they dwell, many having finished their work here below have gone to their reward.

It seems wonderful how one man could exert such an influence for good over so many young people. He always had a kind word to say to every one. He was always commending them for the progress they were making in studies or in public exercises. If any seemed to fail, he would encourage them by telling them that they had done as well or better than some distinguished persons had done in their early efforts. He was constantly inciting them to high and noble deeds, to high and noble lives. He did this in a great measure by setting before them what others had done, how any one could make himself or herself just about what he or she wished. "Where there is a will there is a way," was his motto. He would contrast the lives of the high and noble with the low and debased ; the benevolent with the selfish : those who love to do good with those who injure and degrade their fellow-men.

In the Sunday School, at the close of each session, he was accustomed to make a few remarks, bringing out some point in the lesson, and making a practical application, calculated to lead the sinner to consecrate his life to Christ, or the Christian to give himself more entirely to God's service. He was constantly bringing out the idea that nothing, however great the poverty, or however unfavorable the circumstances, could prevent any one from becoming an eminent servant of God. To illustrate this, he would relate some anecdote. The following, as I remember it, in regard to Jonas King, is one that I have heard him tell two or three times. Rev. Jonas King's grandparents used to live in Oakham. They were so poor they were not able to build a house, but lived under some shelving rocks, and Mr. King's mother was born there under those rocks. They can be seen now, by going out into "Bro. Dean's" wood lot ("Bro. Dean" was my father). The family moved into the west part of the State, and continued very poor. In 1807, when Jonas was fifteen years old, he had such a desire to obtain an education, that one December morning he walked seven miles, to Plainfield, where a Mr. Maynard was teaching. He reached the school-house before the school began. He had no money, nor could his parents help him, and he was a stranger there. But he had such a strong desire to study that Mr. Maynard found a place where he could work for his board, and go to school that winter. In the spring he found a minister who heard him recite while he boarded at home. He worked his way through college, and after some years became a professor in Amherst college, and afterwards became a Foreign Missionary to Greece, and now for many years, has been one of the most distinguished laborers for the welfare of his fellow-men that has lived in our day. Perhaps no one has done more for the cause of education and religion than he. Now no one of you (Deacon Allen would say), has any greater obstacles in the way of obtaining an education, and preparing yourself for usefulness than he had; what Jonas King has done you can do.

Deacon Allen exerted a great influence over the young by seeing that they had the right kind of books to read. He saw to it that the Sunday School had a good library, and was yearly supplied with new books. One of the Merriams, of the Merriam Publishing House, at Springfield, was a great friend of his, and through him he got books at a low price, and no poor book was allowed to go into the library. The reading of these books exerted a great influence over me. In those days this library contained nearly all the books the young people had to read. He watched for souls and took much interest in the temporal welfare of every one, but cared much more for their salvation and spiritual welfare.

His whole being was filled with joy when he saw his loved ones coming to Christ. I well remember his expressions of joy in the spring of 1842, when God so poured out his spirit that a hundred or more of Oakham's young people were brought to

Christ. How he labored for souls during that revival! No one present will ever forget those Sabbath School sessions. For a time he would invite a few to his home every evening whom he knew to be anxious for their soul's salvation. I overheard him say a few weeks after, to a person from another town, that not one of those thus invited left without expressing hope in Christ.

HATFIELD, March 25, 1888.

My earliest memories of Deacon Allen, recall him as teaching me in grammar and arithmetic. I did not feel afraid of him, although he must have been a stern and exacting teacher. He knew when a scholar did his best, and we knew that he delighted in our progress and success, and was fond of showing us off to visitors and in examinations. I think that we did succeed remarkably well, and the reasons for our success were largely found in his way of teaching, and his ability to incite us to eager study. After he ceased teaching, he enjoyed helping at examinations, and nothing pleased him better than to hear rapid and correct solutions of questions in vulgar fractions out of Colburn's Mental Arithmetic. His face would beam as he listened.

All who saw him in the church choir, with his bass viol, knew that he was charmed with sacred music. And the time came when we found that he was best pleased with the singing of children. Lowell Mason began to teach children to sing, and there was great interest aroused on the subject in Boston, and then in the country at large. Deacon Allen was in Boston. I think he was there as a member of the State legislature. He heard a thousand children singing, with Mr. Mason for their leader, and came back to Oakham full of enthusiasm on the subject. He at once gathered the children and taught them to sing together, and not only the children, but everybody enjoyed their singing. Afterwards a new musical instrument was invented. It was about as large as a modern soap box. On its top there were keys, arranged in the order of the keys of a piano, but they were put close together, and were shaped like large pegs. Below, there was a double bellows, and the reeds were between the keyboard and the bellows. The performer put it on his knees or on a table, and made the bellows act by pressing first with one wrist and then with the other, while he also fingered the keys. This was the primitive melodeon, the ancestor of the present American Organ. They were made at Worcester. Deacon Allen bought one of the first that were made, and brought it home in triumph, and he soon had the pleasure of hearing one of his daughters play it, while he and the rest sang. After a while he arranged to have it blown by the foot, having set it in a frame and worked by a strap which was fastened at one end. The girls found it easier to blow it in this way than by pressing with their wrists. Every member of the family was a good singer, and especially Sunday evening they gathered and sang for an hour or two. When at Oakham in vacations, I joined them and sang bass while the Deacon sang tenor, and the rest sang soprano and contralto. It was delightful.

He was very fond of fruit culture. Downing's large work on raising fruit, with its outline figures and careful descriptions, was his text-book and he was ever on the watch for hints and ways of improving his trees and vines. I went with him to prune and scrape and graft an old orchard which he had bought. It was a mile away, so that we had time for talking while going and coming, as well as while at work on the trees. I do not think that any subject but fruit culture was broached. He told me of nice grapevines that he had found which bore grapes of the Catawba shape and flavor, and which he was going to cultivate in his garden, and also of his idea that he could grow cranberries successfully in his garden. Afterwards he showed me both the grapes and the cranberries which he had transplanted, and of which he was enjoying the fruit. He gave what time he could to his garden and orchard, and wished to do more, but his duties as surveyor and as an official servant of the public in various ways, occupied the most of his time. He thought everything of his children, and was very kind to them and regardful of their wishes. But when he learned that Abbie wished to go with me to India, he would not give his consent. She was the oldest left at home, and he said he thought her first duty was to help her younger sisters who had lost their mother. His love for Abbie blinded him, for his second wife was a most judicious and kind step-mother. She sympathized with Abbie's wish to engage in the foreign missionary work, and did it understandingly, as her older sister was Mrs. Bird of the mission to Syria.

5

He continued to refuse his consent for nearly two years. Then he came round and just as decidedly approved of her going, and helped it on. He told me how he was led to change his mind. He said that Rev. Mr. Trask, of Warren, gave them a remarkable sermon on Deut. 32-11, "As an eagle stirreth up her nest," etc. The principal idea of the sermon was that as the eagle made her nest uncomfortable for her young ones when they were ready to fly. but would not, so God stirred up their nest for them when his people refused to do their duty. "And," said the deacon, "it came to me very plainly that my nest had been stirred up, and I made up my mind that I would oppose the will of God no longer. And now I will help Abbie to go."

As Abbie lived only six years in India, I thought that he might, after all. think that her going had been a mistake. So when I met him again. I asked him about it. He said that he thought she had probably lived longer there than she would had she remained in America. But whatever might have been the result, he had never for a moment regretted her going.

S. B. FAIRBANK.

Daniel H. Parker, of Dunbarton, N. H., says: "I am glad you have undertaken the writing of a life history of Deacon Allen. I think of him as a model man who engaged in every good work and finished well whatever he undertook."

Mr. Henry Clapp, once a boy in Oakham, now in business in Chicago, says: "One of my most distinct recollections of Deacon Allen is that he never liked to see any one standing around whether at school. at church, or elsewhere, and when he passed such persons he advised them to move on, and find something to do, or at least make their appearance not as *idlers* but as those who at least *wanted* something to do. And he used to caution people about stopping to talk in the doorways, saying that doorways were made for ingress and egress and not for stopping places, and no well-bred person would use them as such."

Mrs. Reliance Kendall, of Cambridgeport, Mass. (a daughter of Deacon Solomon Crocker), says, in a letter of April 27, 1888: "A strong and intimate friendship existed between my father and his brother-in-law Deacon James Allen. That was the principal reason that led him to locate in Oakham; that he might be near one whose society he so much valued and who was more to him really than a brother. I remember him as a great lover of children, and they fully reciprocated his love. Nothing pleased us more than to see him approaching the house;—he was always greeted with delight. He delighted in music and he devoted a great deal of his time in teaching the children to sing;—he sang a great deal in his home with his children. It was my privilege to spend a few weeks in his family, and I shall remember with pleasure to my latest day the many happy seasons we had singing together, while uncle played the bass-viol. I saw Uncle Allen but very little after I was thirteen years of age, but I used to hear my mother speak of him so often, and with what I knew of him personally I knew that he was an exceptionally good and useful man, prominent in every good work. I hope I shall have the privilege of owning the book when it is completed."

OAKHAM, April 6, 1888.

It was not my privilege to be a pupil of Deacon Allen, in the public school, nor to be with him much in the daily walks of life, but as far as I have been, he impressed me both by precept and example as the right type of a man, always safe to follow.

I am aware that others can speak of his business tact and talent better than I can. But perhaps I may speak of him more in the line of Church and Sunday School work. I feel very grateful for the interest he took in the young people, of whom I was one. Well do I remember the year 1842, when we were blessed with an outpouring of God's Spirit; what kind and fatherly care he exercised in gathering the converts at his house for a morning prayer meeting. Many a one's thoughts go back to Deacon Allen's morning prayer meeting and feel that there they got started in the right way. His Sabbath School work will be remembered as long as life lasts, and the yielding up of those positions which he held so long and faithfully, with so much grace and cheerfulness, had its impression upon those who followed him. The encouragement which he gave to others who were bearing heavy burdens was characteristic of him and very helpful to them.

He stood like a good soldier at his post doing what he could; and when he was called to go, he expressed to his friends that it was not in anything he had done that he trusted, but in the mercy of Christ; and we could all feel that he had gone up higher.

JAMES PACKARD.

BOSTON, June 14, 1888.

DEAR MR. KNIGHT:

When I received your circular, several weeks ago, asking me to contribute in some way to the work which you had in contemplation, I did not respond for the reason that I did not feel competent to write anything which could add interest to the "Life History," which I was very glad to know was to be written. On receiving the second circular, I thought that perhaps I had not been true to my own convictions of duty in remaining silent. * *

Deacon James Allen was one of "Nature's Noblemen" in the truest and best sense of the term, and as the years roll on, I think we realize the fact more and more, for how few men do we see who possess the rare gifts which shone in his character, or, possessing them, will devote them unreservedly to the work of benefiting others and blessing mankind. His entire character seems to have been made up of noble traits and qualities, either one of which, when studied and analyzed, seems only to give brighter lustre to his memory. His name seems to me to be associated with all that is *noble* and *true*, and the influence of his words and example while living will be a power in the town in which he lived, and in other communities for many years to come. My remembrance of Deacon Allen is perhaps more vivid and impressive while he was a teacher, and a little later a supervisor of the schools in Oakham.

His manner of teaching was peculiarly his own;—with great tact and keen discernment he would lead his pupils to realize the importance of making the *most* of whatever talent or ability they might possess, at the same time commanding their highest respect and esteem; patient and faithful in illustrating and explaining the particular lesson under consideration, and whenever an opportunity occurred never failed to bring to bear on the minds of his class, some *moral lesson* which, whatever else they might forget, would cling to their memory and leave its influence in after life. The interest which he seemed to feel in his pupils was *remarkable*, more like that of a father for his children ;— nor did it cease when the school-days ended, but followed them as they left the home of their youth, to assume new cares and duties, with his *benediction* and *prayers;* and if by chance they should after a time return to their childhood home and revisit the friends of earlier years, who ever gave them a heartier welcome to the town, or a more cordial greeting than the dear old teacher?

I think as an instructor of the young Deacon Allen was far in *advance* of the *times* in which he taught, and when I think of the innovations, the *new methods* and *improvements so called*, in teaching to-day which may be more ornamental but *far* less practical and helpful to a young person who has to meet life as it comes to us all, my thoughts revert with *great satisfaction* to the common sense style of Deacon James Allen, the *model teacher.*

You will please accept what I have imperfectly written, as the honest expression of my heart, and sincere tribute to the memory of my beloved teacher, benefactor and friend.

Yours very truly.

CLARINDA R. ELLIS (*née* ADAMS).

From Deacon Albert Spooner of North Brookfield.

Deacon Allen was my nearest neighbor during my boyhood, and was ever regarded as a natural guardian of the public morals and a worthy example of obedience to his convictions. From my earliest recollections he was associated with my father as deacon of the church and always the leading spirit. A self-constituted monitor of decorum at church or other meetings ; one whose advice and counsel was often sought and cheerfully given on various subjects.

I remember him as my teacher in the public schools and in the High School. One interesting recollection is that in my early school days he had a library of Peter Parley's and other books, which he loaned to the scholars ; it was regarded as quite a favor in those days, and cultivated a love for reading and a desire for knowledge.

But perhaps the most endearing memory of his life was in the winter and spring of 1842, in that extensive revival of religion, when he gathered those of us who had just been born into the kingdom, into his parlor and learned us the first words of prayer that we had ever used in the presence of others; those sunrise meetings we enjoyed there for weeks;—their memory seems like hallowed ground, and his patriarchal share in them may well incite us to say *blessed be his memory.* And when we shall greet him in heavenly mansions and review these rich experiences we'll strike our harps anew in praise of Him who bought us with His blood and led us in these heavenly ways.

MINNEAPOLIS, Minn., June 6, 1888.

MR. HIRAM KNIGHT, *Dear Sir:*

I received your "Friendly Greeting" in due time. Please excuse my long delay in answering. You ask me to give you some of my recollections of Deacon James Allen. Memory carries me back more than fifty years to the time when I first knew him. I was a mere boy, not more than twelve years old. He was then deacon of the church in Oakham, and one of its most earnest and efficient members, also superintendent of the Sunday School. I well remember him as teacher in the public schools. He was town clerk for many years, and served the town from time to time as selectman and assessor. He also represented the town in the legislature, and held the office of County Commissioner for several years. He was always interested in the welfare of the *young*, and in everything pertaining to the best interests of the town he always manifested a lively interest and took an active part.

I can truly say that in all the relations of life, as husband, father, teacher, or public officer he was a model Christian man. And when his life work was done (like a shock of corn fully ripe and ready for the harvest) he passed on to the higher life, to his reward in *heaven.*

Yours Truly,

J. W. BRIGHAM.

OBERLIN, O., June 12, 1888.

H. KNIGHT, Esq., *Dear Sir:*

I fully intended on receiving your circular to write and say that I should be glad to receive the book and to add some of my personal reminiscences of one whom we all delight to honor. My first remembrance of Deacon Allen was of his teaching a singing school for little children. Some one sang out of time and tune, which caused a laugh among the others, and brought tears to the eyes of the child. The mild reproof administered to those who laughed did not affect me so much as the ready sympathy shown to the timid, sensitive girl, who but for the kind encouraging word and look would probably never have ventured to sing again. Deacon Allen was fond of music, and for many years led the choir in the old church accompanied by his bass viol.

I recall many a Sabbath afternoon when he gathered his family around him and sang the tunes he loved so well:— "Gently Lord, O gently lead us." "There is a fountain filled with blood." "False are the men of high degree." "There is a stream whose gentle flow." These hymns always bring Deacon Allen and his bass viol and those quiet Sunday evening hours fresh to my mind. In the Sunday School, in the day school, in the garden, or on the street he commanded the love and respect of all who knew him. He rejoiced in the successes of others and sympathized with the unfortunate. He would not tolerate sin or wrong in any one, but was kind and gentle towards the repentant and ever ready by word and deed to restore such to favor. His regard for woman was great,—many a young man has occasion to thank Deacon Allen for reproof or advice in regard to his treatment of mother, sister or schoolmate. Equally fortunate were the girls who were members of his school for the fatherly counsels and warnings given. One remark of his which has always been fresh in my memory, "A lady may always know in what estimation she is held by the other sex by the language he addresses to her."

Deacon Allen was dignified but always courteous, even to the poor and humble. He commanded respect because he was worthy of it. Time would fail me to record all the pleasant memories of the grand, good man. In June, 1851, I bade him good-bye for the last time. He did not then seem to me like an old man. I received several kind, affectionate letters from him; from his death-bed he sent me loving messages. I shall always cherish next to Mr. Kimball and my own kindred the memory of Deacon James Allen, and never cease to thank God for the holy and blessed influence of his life on me and the community around. May his mantle fall on all who bear his name. The judgment alone will reveal the good he did in life. "Yea his works do follow him." With kind regards,

Believe me yours truly,

L. W. MELLEN (née Fairbank).

DEACON JAMES ALLEN.

Many are the pleasant memories I have of Deacon James Allen; not so much of definite facts, to which I can affix an exact date, as of a general all pervasive influence for good, a delightful fragrance which penetrated my life, as it did that of the town and church, and whose blessed influence will never lose its power. The whole community in which he dwelt can say of him what Tennyson wrote of his friend—

> " Whatever way my days decline
> I felt and feel tho' left alone,
> His being working in my own
> The footsteps of his life in mine."

He was well on in life when I went to Oakham to be pastor of the Congregational Church. He had already resigned his position as superintendent of the Sunday School which he had held for over forty years, because, as he told me, he would not hold it till he became too old to perceive that he ought to resign; telling the story of the judge who resigned his position at sixty, but was overpersuaded to continue in office since every one wished him so to do; he was in the perfection of his powers; and then when he was very old and really failing, and friends suggested that it would be well to surrender his duties to younger hands, he utterly refused, because "he was never better able to fulfil his duties than at that hour."

But Deacon Allen never lost his influence. He loved the church as the apple of his eye, and his judgment was held in the highest esteem. He was a very firm man, but it was the firmness not so much of a granite rock, as of an oak tree with elastic branches and touching others with flexible twigs and delicate leaves. So that he would give up his will rather than injure the church in any way. He was not one of those "who wish the Lord's will to be done, but always want to be on the committee of ways and means." To illustrate his own position he used to tell me the story of the very obstinate man who refused to yield to the majority because his conscience would not let him. But what is your conscience? Why it is something in here that says, "I won't, I won't." His love for the church always conquered self, and this victory was very manifest in all that he did. It seemed almost that as Queen Mary declared that after her death "Calais" would be found written on her heart, so on his heart of hearts was written "The cause of God in Oakham, and the world." He was absolutely to be depended upon to stand up for the right.

At one period of my ministry in Oakham a young man wished to join the church and it had been voted by the church to receive him. But he was not satisfied with his baptism in infancy, and wished to be baptized on admission to the church. I told him that I would do it, for it was clear to me that while re-baptism was unnecessary, and contrary to the meaning of baptism, yet every person ought to be satisfied in his own mind that he was baptized once. My duty was to satisfy his conscience rather than my own. But Saturday afternoon Deacon Allen came to the parsonage and enquired whether the report was true, and objected to the re-baptism. We agreed to put the matter off till the next communion. In the meantime each of us wrote to leading influential ministers stating the case and asking information. We read the letters to one another; we had a discussion before the whole church, and the church voted as one of its principles that it favored such adult baptism. Deacon Allen also voted for it, but added to the vote the statement that in such a case the candidate should give unusual proofs of his religious character. There was not the least friction or hard feeling, but we both seemed drawn nearer to each other than before.

The Deacon was strongly inclined to the Old School views of

Christian doctrine. In the Pan-Presbyterian Assembly in Scotland some twenty years ago, two of the American delegates were asked to define the difference between the Old School and the New. One took an hour or two to define the difference, when the other said that he thought he could state the difference in much briefer form; the Old School men believed

> "In Adam's fall
> We sinned all,"

while the New School men believed

> "In Adam's fall
> We all sinned,"

the difference being that they did not like the doctrine so well as to put it in rhyme and sing it. I think Deacon Allen would put it in rhyme and sing it. And yet he was a decidedly progressive man. He did not "sit on the tail of progress and halloo whoa."

He was always looking forward, seeking better and larger things. His contact with the world outside of his native town, and with men of influence and power broadened his vision and enlarged his sympathies. To him the good of yesterday was "the standing place of to-day," but he never took his foot from its present position till he saw some firm ground in advance on which to plant it.

Deacon Allen was one of the kindest hearted men I ever knew. It was to his house that I and my little family came on the cold December day that we entered the town to make it our home. The welcome was warm, the hospitality generous.

> "He kept his climate in his heart
> And it was Summer there."

He always stood by his pastor. He was treasurer of the church, and was one of the best and most faithful treasurers. It is very difficult to express how much we owe of our usefulness and happiness while we were in Oakham to the loving kindness of the Deacon and his family. I kept a memoranda of all the little love-gifts made to us from the parish, and a great number of them came from him and his. And it will be one of my first privileges in heaven to seek him out, and express to him with an angel's tongue, what this mortal tongue is unable to express, our grateful love for his example, his manhood, his help and his kindness to the young minister who preached to him from the pulpit, but who all the week sat at his feet to learn from his noble character.

Most truly yours,

F. N. PELOUBET.

NATICK, MASS., July 27, 1888.

From Rev. George H. Gould, D.D., writing from Paxton, August 6, 1888.

As I turn back to my boyhood days no figure stands out more prominently and luminously on the horizon of memory than that of Deacon James Allen. He was part and parcel at that time of the whole religious, educational and political ongoing of my native town. He easily distanced all competitors as our foremost citizen. And yet he put on no airs. He assumed no superiority. In manner and speech he was simple as a child. He was as companionable with a boy of fifteen as with a man of fifty. But no one could casually meet him and not be impressed instantly with his native dignity and almost courtly refinement of manner. He was a nobleman in homespun. In Nature's heraldry he was a prince of the blood. He was as instinctively a gentleman at the plough or trudging on foot with his surveyor's implements, as when acting his part as legislator in the Senate Chamber of the Commonwealth.

He was a natural teacher. He loved the vocation. He left his personal impress as an educator on more than a whole generation of the population of the town. Equally he loved to acquire and to impart knowledge. An enthusiast in whatever he put his hand to, his own subtle and delicate enthusiasm always set his pupils on fire. He was no less prominent as a religious teacher,—next to the minister he was the leading man in the church. If the minister was Moses, he was Aaron, true yokefellow. If the minister was David, he was Joab, leader of the royal host. And to this position, without a thought of jealousy on the part of others, by his real weight and worth he gravitated as naturally as a river runs to the sea. Nor did one ever think of grudging him any honor he wore, political or churchwise, so modestly and sympathetically did he wear all his honors in the service of others.

There are two pictures I carry in my boyish mind of Deacon Allen, after this lapse of half a century, which perhaps stand out more distinctly than any others. And both are connected with the old meeting-house and its Sunday services. The first is as he sat in the high gallery fronting the pulpit, at the head of the choir, leading the "service of song," with his bass viol—the soul of that bass viol and his own soul seemed to have an especial affinity for each other. He fingered it as gently and pressed it to his side as fondly, while drawing sweet strains from its inner depths, as if it had been a part of himself. He was a true devotee of music—not of the boisterous, clashing or riotous kind, but of the sweet, tender and aeolian type—seeking to express all the deeper and subtler melodies of the soul, in an uplift of true worship before God. Indeed, I think my first conception of worshipful music came from Deacon Allen. His soul was strung to the finest spiritual harmonies. He seemed lifted up to new heights of religious vision the moment he began to sing. His exquisite song-gift thus became, whenever in exercise, a kind of transfiguration of the whole man.

One of his favorite tunes was "Greenville," and in the single "Fall Term" I was privileged to be his pupil, no reminiscence of that term, or, indeed, of the fifty years since fled, lives more sacredly and imperishably in my memory to-day, than the echoes of that tune, sung by all the scholars at the close of each day's session, accompanied by the words,

> "Lord dismiss us with thy blessing,
> Fill our hearts with joy and peace."

Fortunate for Deacon Allen's Puritan conscience and peace of soul, that he lived before wise Civilians at this later era have discovered, that the Bible and the religion of Christ are too dangerous and sectarian matters to be allowed any place in the daily instruction of the young. The second picture of the good deacon, church-wise, to which I refer, was his position at the head of the Sunday School, as superintendent, covering a period I think from first to last of some forty years. In some important respects I have never yet seen Deacon Allen surpassed as a Sunday-school superintendent. He lived, it is true, before the day of trained experts in that office. He doubtless would have been a clumsy manipulator of all the ropes and wires by which certain modern schools are run. In fact, he was not a mechanician at all. He was a living presence, a personal power. Taken by himself, he was preëminently an object lesson of sweet, noble and self-poised Christian manliness, as he stood up each Sunday before the whole school. As the sap fills and vivifies the whole tree to its remotest twig, so his majestic personality filled and stimulated the farthest class in the room. He was not a profuse talker—he had nothing of the bustling officiousness of a mere drill-master. It was his custom at the close of the hour to throw open the school for questions and free interchange of views on the hard points of the lesson. In this exercise he had a rare gift of leadership. His own voice, as I remember it, during this brief composium was sweet as the notes of a flute, while his face was full of sunshine. His manner was gracious and patient with the most obtuse questioner, and while settled in his own convictions as the granite hills, he was ever tolerant and generous towards all honest doubt and difficulty. He was not especially a " children's man," in the modern sense of that phrase. He was only a moderate story-teller. He never " gushed " or sentimentalized. He never talked down to his audience, but old and young alike were charmed and edified by the intrinsic lucidity and unstilted *naturalness* of all that he said. * * * *

I have laid emphasis on the genial and winsome side of Deacon Allen's character, but before I leave the old meeting-house I must refer to an incident that gave the present writer a sudden and memorable flash of insight into another side of the man's make-up. It was the habit of a group of boys just entering their " teens," of whom myself was one, untethered to any parental pew or oversight on the ground floor of the church, to install ourselves during preaching service in some one of the spacious and for the most part unoccupied square pews that ran around the whole outer edge of the lofty gallery above. On a certain Sunday a party of us roving and uncircumcised urchins chanced to occupy a pew at the extreme end of the gallery, and directly over against the pulpit. As the solemn service progressed, some scamp of a boy in our circle, overcome with profane and most mistimed merriment, let slip a snicker, so loud that it startled the whole congregation, and instantly every eye turned towards the offending quarter—A moment's pause—Then uprose the tall form of Deacon Allen, seeming to our alarmed gaze like Mt. Sinai, as he slowly straightened himself up, his eyes flashing fire and his brow clothed with tempest—in sight of the whole transfixed audience, deliberately and majestically he bent his measured steps along the lengthy passage-way to our conspicuous and doomed pew. Swinging wide the door, without a word he took his seat in the midst of the trembling band of culprits. A silence like the grave reigned in that pew until the service closed, when a few words were spoken of such incisive reproof and righteous severity that the ears of one offender at least, after fifty years, still tingle at their memory.

But only a year or two after this unseemly side-play of youthful irreverence in the house of God, comes a period covering several months—months now sacred and precious in retrospect almost beyond any bygone experiences of earth. In that experience so hallowed and delightful to recall, Deacon Allen figured most prominently.

It was the occasion of a great and notable work of grace stirring the whole town, largely among the young, when more than fifty on a single Sabbath in the old church stood up in confession of a new found Christian hope. Never shall I forget the "sunrise prayer meeting" inaugurated at that juncture by Deacon Allen and held daily for weeks at his own house,—where like a tender shepherd he took the young lambs in his arms, strengthened their trembling faith, and gradually brought them out into green pastures of God, and into a wider and richer experience of his saving love and power.   *   *   *

But no sketch of Deacon Allen would be complete that made no reference to his almost passionate love for horticulture,—like religion and music it stirred the profoundest sentiments of his nature. Every tree bearing fruit, it could almost be said, in his eyes, was a "tree of life" with its home on the banks of some river that flowed fast by the throne of God. His garden was to him indeed " paradise regained," where at intervals of more toilsome labor, he spent many of his happiest hours. Along no channels did the stream of his sparkling and quenchless enthusiasm run higher than here. He petted and coddled his trees almost as if of his own flesh and blood. Their growth and outshoots of promise and good behavior from year to year filled him with exquisite delight. A dull boy was he in the whole neighborhood, if straying occasionally into the deacon's garden, who did not learn from his eloquent lips the pedigree, foreign or otherwise, of every fruit-bearer on the premises.

In a letter from George C. Ripley, Esq., 164 Hicks Street, Brooklyn, N. Y., president of the Home Life Insurance Company of New York, dated August 22, 1888, he says :—

It affords me great pleasure at this late day to thank you for the opportunity of obtaining a partial history of Oakham, "My own, my native land" (town).

> " Lives there a man with soul so dead
> Who never to himself hath said,
> This is," &c.

The name of Deacon James Allen is very dear to me (possibly from the fact of blood relationship though remote). My grandmother on my father's side was a sister of Captain Washington Allen (who was a cousin of James, I think). It was he who, with Stephen Lincoln, canvassed the town for children to attend a Sunday School in about 1819 (1818), and I was the only one from the little North Village (now Coldbrook), who attended the organization the first Sabbath in May of that year.

Both Deacon Allen and Mr. Lincoln were my long-lived friends, and the *latter* with his family were everything to me in my orphanage that parents could have been.

www.ingramcontent.com/pod-product-compliance
Lightning Source LLC
Chambersburg PA
CBHW031241260626
47169CB00007B/2409